Stories by Contemporary Writers from Shanghai

# PLATINUM
# PASSPORT

This book is edited and designed by the Editorial Committee of *Cultural China* series

Text by Zhu Xiaolin
Translation by Jiang Yajun, Zhu Ping
Cover Image by Getty Images
Interior Design by Xue Wenqing
Cover Design by Wang Wei

Editors: Wu Yuezhou, Susan Luu Xiang
Editorial Director: Zhang Yicong

Senior Consultants: Sun Yong, Wu Ying, Yang Xinci
Managing Director and Publisher: Wang Youbu

ISBN: 978-1-60220-240-5

Address any comments about *Platinum Passport* to:

Better Link Press
99 Park Ave
New York, NY 10016
USA

or

Shanghai Press and Publishing Development Company
F 7 Donghu Road, Shanghai, China (200031)
Email: comments_betterlinkpress@hotmail.com

Printed in China by Shanghai Donnelley Printing Co., Ltd.

1   3   5   7   9   10   8   6   4   2

# PLATINUM PASSPORT

By Zhu Xiaolin

Better Link Press

# Foreword

This collection of books for English readers consists of short stories and novellas published by writers based in Shanghai. Apart from a few who are immigrants to Shanghai, most of them were born in the city, from the latter part of the 1940s to the 1980s. Some of them had their works published in the late 1970s and the early 1980s; some gained recognition only in the 21st century. The older among them were the focus of the "To the Mountains and Villages" campaign in their youth, and as a result, lived and worked in the villages. The difficult paths of their lives had given them unique experiences and perspectives prior to their eventual return to Shanghai. They took up creative writing for different reasons but all share a creative urge and a love for writing. By profession, some of them are college professors, some literary editors, some directors of literary institutions, some freelance writers and some professional writers. From the individual styles of the authors and the art of their writings, readers can easily detect traces of the authors' own experiences in life, their interests, as well as their aesthetic values. Most of the works in this collection are still written in the realistic style that represents, in a painstakingly fashioned fictional world, the changes of the times in urban and rural life. Having grown up in a more open era, the younger writers have been spared the hardships experienced by their predecessors, and therefore seek greater freedom in their writing. Whatever category of writers they belong to, all of them have gained their rightful places in the Chinese literary circles over the last forty years. Shanghai writers tend to favor urban narratives more than other genres of writing. Most of the works in this collection can be characterized as urban literature with Shanghai characteristics, but there are also exceptions.

Called the "Paris of the East," Shanghai was already an international metropolis in the 1920s and 30s. Being the center of China's economy, culture and literature at the time, it housed a majority of writers of importance in the history of modern Chinese literature. The list includes Lu Xun, Guo Moruo, Mao Dun and Ba Jin, who had all written and published prolifically in Shanghai. Now, with Shanghai re-emerging as a globalized metropolis, the Shanghai writers who have appeared on the literary scene in the last forty years all face new challenges and literary quests of the times. I am confident that some of the older writers will produce new masterpieces. As for the fledging new generation of writers, we naturally expect them to go far in their long writing careers ahead of them. In due course, we will also introduce those writers who did not make it into this collection.

Wang Jiren
Series Editor

# Contents

# Platinum Passport

# I

In two years, three young women lecturers in the School of Languages at F University "ran away." The staff in the school coined the phrase to refer to those who go abroad to study or work at the university's expense but never return. The three unmarried lecturers were enrolled at Confucius Schools in America. The first wrote a letter of resignation when her contract expired; the other two went even further by sending express mails to resign from the university at the Shanghai Pudong Airport before their plane took off, giving the dean of the school a surprise when their planes touched down at the airports in America.

It must be much less surprising to the dean if it had happened twenty years ago in China, when poverty was the driving force behind similar decisions. The several professors at the school who returned from abroad in the last two decades of the last century could swap stories about their life abroad for hours and hours. If Chinese university professors are paid as much as they were twenty years ago and still live in apartments like barracks, why should they choose to be "returnees"? After all, patriotism can never be economically baseless.

Before the winter holiday, Professor Lu Jianhua, a returnee from America, complained at the last staff meeting. "These young ladies don't know what they are doing. They must think the streets of America are paved with money. They are dreaming. It's not wise at all to resign when you are decent university lecturers in China. What's the good in ending up as American housewives?" Holding a doctoral degree from an American university, Professor Lu was one of the leading professors in the country in the field of applied linguistics. As the academic leader at the college, he supervised doctoral students, but above all, his words carried weight and his colleagues seldom argued with him.

Xie Rufang did not agree with Professor Lu's opinion about the "runaway" women, but she remained silent. She was quite familiar with the three women since she lived with them in the same university apartment building for the unmarried staff. With master and doctoral degrees in their hands, they were not ignorant about the United States as to choose to stay there for the easy money. But as a pupil of Professor Lu for her doctoral research, she would never challenge her supervisor. More importantly, it was through his mentoring that she was able to beat out other candidates in joining the university as a young recruit, to which she had been grateful. So instead, she said: "Professor Lu, if they were 'Professors B & A' like you, I don't think they would have decided otherwise."

Professor Lu was nicknamed "Professor B & A" because he was the first at the college to own a Buick and a house in an affluent neighborhood in the city. Rather than being offended, the professor seemed to be pleased about the name. He laughed loudly and made fun of himself. "It sounds as if I'm a corrupt government official who is under investigation for suspected bribery." He was glad that his student mentioned his nickname before his colleagues, so that the conversation could turn to luxurious houses and fancy cars, at which his college staff, especially the young members, looked with envy. The current university professors in China were not only academic tutors and moral examples for their students, their way of living were admired and respected by their students and young colleagues.

Rufang herself was greatly impressed with her professor's Western manners even when she was his doctoral student. When entering a building, he would hold the door to allow ladies to go in first. He would say "excuse me" when he had to sneeze around his students. Those manners were so deeply rooted in him that he would do the same even when he was alone. His experience in America made him a different person, in lifestyle and in mannerism, from his Chinese countrymen. To Rufang, those differences were sometimes more attractive than the measure of money.

Professor Lu stopped Rufang when the staff meeting was over. "Can you order a meal for six from Another Village? I have to play host to a former schoolmate who is back from the U.S. I'll be glad if you and the others can come with me."

Another Village was a restaurant on the university campus. As the costs of the meals at the restaurant were written off as research expense, it had become a popular place for entertaining guests for the professors who had a research budget. Rufang knew that "you and the others" would include herself and his other doctoral students who were often asked to accompany the professor when he had guests. His family had never been invited for these gatherings.

The professor and his four students had been chatting for quite a long time and emptied a nice pot of green tea, but the guest, Zhong Kun, had yet to arrive. The professor felt he had to explain. "This is one of my former schoolmates who have been in the U.S. for more than twenty years. When he's back in China, he refuses to use a taxi and prefers public transportation. You know how terrible the traffic is? God knows where he is now." Soon after, his cell phone rang. It was Zhong Kun asking for help because he missed his stop and couldn't find a return bus.

The professor laughed. "Old Zhong, why don't you take a taxi? Using it occasionally won't do much harm to the environment." He winked at his students after his phone call ended. "Mr. Zhong is an American citizen and he isn't stingy with money for a taxi. He's just an environmentalist." Understanding their professor, the students laughed loudly along with him.

When the guest was finally led into the private room, a third pot of tea had been finished. Compared with the well-dressed Professor Lu, Zhong Kun was rather short and his wrinkled old-fashioned tweed jacket made him look like a shrunken man. No sooner had he seated himself than he reached the cold dishes with his chopsticks without waiting for a "please" from anyone present. His informal American style reversed the duties of the host and the guest, and Professor Lu had to tell his students to start eating.

The guest finally put down his chopsticks to leisurely light up his cigarette as the main courses were served. "The Chinese dishes are always very much to my taste. A couple of tasty meals can be a fair exchange for a flight of more than ten hours across the Pacific," he exclaimed before taking a puff from his cigarette.

"Why don't you cook at home?" Professor Lu asked. "You were the much praised Chinese cook among the Chinese students when I was in the U.S."

Zhong Kun drained a large glass of beer in one gulp before putting his arm on his old classmate's shoulder. "Tell you what, Old Lu, I've been the owner of ten houses in the past few years and a landlord to nine of them. I have to go to each of the renters for the rent. I simply don't have the time to cook."

With those words, Zhong Kun quieted the professor and his students, all of whom were too surprised to say anything. While the professor enjoyed his affluent lifestyle, Rufang and her fellow students lived in the university apartment buildings for the young staff members, or paid rent out of their own pockets if they lived outside the campus. They wondered how a person could afford ten houses.

Zhong Kun was pleased to see what he had wanted to see. While swallowing down a fatty piece of roast duck, he turned to Rufang, from whose face he detected an expression of surprise as well as envy. "That's America, heaven on the earth," he said, looking straight into her eyes.

# II

For the first time in three years, Rufang decided to spend the Spring Festival holiday with her parents in Zhejiang, a neighboring province of Shanghai. Su Yang accompanied her to the railway station even though two hours later he would be in a bus going to his parents' home in Anhui Province. The two met at the Doctoral Forum on campus when Rufang was a PhD student of linguistics and Su Yang worked as a postdoc in the School of Resources and Environment. As for their academic majors, they did not have much in common between them. Rufang knew that they hang out now and then simply because both of them were single and not seeing anyone else.

As women were traditionally expected to get married in their early twenties, the marriage of the thirty-year-old Rufang had been at the top of the agenda for her family, including her brother, sister-in-law, and their children. They expected to see a young man accompany Rufang back home because they had not seen her for more than three years. She knew she would leave her whole family disappointed again.

Knowing Rufang would be embarrassed by questions from the family, her sister-in-law took her baggage with a warm smile in her eyes. "Rufang, you're back home at last. Caiqing came over several times looking for you. She gave birth to a baby boy, the second in the family, and it is American. She's giving away chocolate candy all over the place. You've been close since you were kids. Why don't you go get some of that candy?" She winked at Rufang and then at her mother.

Rufang knew well that her family must have been talking about her marriage before she arrived. Her mother would be greatly disappointed when she learned she was still alone with no boyfriend. The family's Spring Festival gathering would be spoiled and she would be the one to blame. As soon as her sister-in-law took the baggage, Rufang turned and ran off.

Caiqing had gotten married when Rufang was a sophomore at university, and her husband, who was ten years older, was an astute wholesaler of building materials. Rufang knew that their daughter was old enough to go to school. The husband was becoming more successful and he was yearning for a son to continue his business. He was rich and the penalty for breaching the one-child policy was nothing to him. But Rufang wondered how Caiqing came to have an American son. Ever since her husband had a huge three-story house built in the village, it had been the whole world for Caiqing. Was it possible for her to hang out with an American guy? While thinking how ridiculous it could be, she was before the gate of the fancy house. A girl in a red coat cheered when she saw her. "Aunt Rufang is here! Aunt Rufang is here!" Rufang then realized it was Caiqing's daughter.

Hearing the noise, Caiqing rushed out of the yard and hugged her friend, a greeting seldom seen between Chinese friends, which reminded Rufang of her friend's American son. The mom of an American son hugs her friends, Rufang thought.

"Where's your son?" Rufang asked as she struggled out of Caiqing's arms. "How can a Chinese mom give birth to an American baby? Does it have blond hair and blue eyes?"

Caiqing patted Rufang's shoulder. "Blond hair and blue eyes? What're you talking about? It's our own natural son, but he has an American passport. By law, he's American. My son is an American citizen, and of course I'm the mom of an American boy."

Caiqing was four months pregnant when her husband was told by his women business partners, who had gotten rich from doing deals with him, that they could choose Saipan, an unincorporated territory of the United States in the western Pacific Ocean, as the birth place of their second child. The choice would save them from paying the penalty for having a second child in China, and the child would be an American citizen according to the American practice of citizenship by birth if it was born on the island. Furthermore, they could have as many children as they wished. Caiqing discussed with her husband and they signed a contract with an "American baby" agent, which helped them with the formalities ranging from the visa to the hospital to the passport. They paid a total of fifty thousand yuan(1 U.S. dollar is about 6.1 yuan) and the child was born later on the American island territory.

Caiqing's husband told everyone that the business paid for itself. The baby was American by law, Caiqing was not fined, and she and her husband would be granted green cards when their son turned eighteen. Now that Caiqing and her husband had a newborn American baby, the villagers began to look up to them, because they knew it was a wealthy country and it was an honor to be connected with it.

Wrapped in a bright blanket, the baby was sucking his own fingers while searching the ceiling with his black eyes. Everything was new to him. What he did not know was that his birth certificate and passport had been put in an exquisite frame so that they could be shown to guests without any damage done to it.

Handing the frame over to Rufang, Caiqing said: "You have a doctoral degree, so you can tell the value of this passport. The guys at the agency told us Chinese passports are made of paper, but American ones are made of platinum."

"I think this American passport is also made of paper," Rufang said, pretending not to understand what her friend meant.

Caiqing's husband cut in. "You can go wherever you want with an American passport, but you have to apply for a visa for any country if you have a Chinese one. That's the difference between a paper and a platinum passport."

Rufang forced a smile and did not continue the conversation. She spent more than twenty years in school and university and she had a doctoral degree, but she had never been abroad. The topic would leave her in an embarrassing situation.

It was a sleepless night for her. Her parents had more rooms and the one she was in had never been used in the past three years. It seemed the floor and the wall smelled musty, a smell that prevented her from getting to sleep. She then put her hands under her head and opened her eyes. What she saw during the day popped into her head and she felt a pang of envy at her friend Caiqing for her lovely children, the three-story house, and the framed American passport. She had never thought of Caiqing when she was in her apartment room in Shanghai, and Caiqing, who dropped out of school, was the last person for her to be jealous of, although she was married to a wealthy man. She never knew if Caiqing was ever jealous of her degree and her profession as a university teacher, but Rufang was certain that she longed for Caiqing's life, a comfortable life with a couple of children.

She stayed late on Chinese New Year's Eve to set off string after string of firecrackers with her nephews. She was awoken by a New Year text message from Su Yang. Touched by his solicitude for her on the first day of the New Year, she began to text back while lying beneath the covers. She edited the message again and again to hide her excitement, because she thought a woman should be shy and reserved with a man. But she regretted the words the moment they were sent. How could she ignore a man she met while envying Caiqing's life? Su Yang was the male friend with whom she had been for the longest time in her life. She then texted him again, saying it was hard for her to search for materials for her research project as she had no access to the Internet in her village. She hoped her second message could strike a balance between the indifference in the first and an expression of affection for him.

Su Yang responded with a string of text messages. He had no access to the Internet at home either and he had to ride a bicycle to the nearest town that was more than ten kilometers away. He would sit in the Internet bar for hours every day. He said that he had an important matter to discuss with her and suggested that she return to the university earlier.

Rufang could feel her heart pounding in her chest. Has the shy guy drummed up his courage to propose to her? What else could be so urgent that she had to go back early? She kissed her cell phone, but decided not to respond to his message immediately. The next day she told Su Yang that she would go back to Shanghai on the fifth day of the first Chinese month, but only because she needed the university online database to finish one of her research articles. She wanted Su Yang to know that her decision was because of her research project rather than his suggestion.

It was tradition that the Chinese Spring Festival end on the fifteenth of the month, but she booked a return ticket for the fifth without telling her family. Her mother was not happy about her decision. "It's the first visit in three years. Why can't you stay longer? After all, you don't have a boyfriend back in Shanghai." Rufang did not answered back as she often did when her mother nagged at her, but put her arms around her mother's neck. "I'm not going to waste my time at home with you. I'm going back to look for a husband."

Her sister-in-law smiled. "My dear sister, when you get a boyfriend, make sure to bring him back to meet our parents. Matters of marriage can't be decided by you alone, can they?"

Her older brother, who seldom joked with her, patted the back of her head. "A woman doesn't have to be so well-educated. Guys don't like women with glasses."

Rufang tried to kick her brother for the joke, but she knew all the family was concerned about her marriage prospects as she was already thirty years old. Without saying goodbye to Caiqing and her other friends in the village, she rushed back to the city.

## III

Su Yang told Rufang in a text message he was waiting for her at "the usual place," a small square with a huge marble statue in the center of Mao Zedong, the founding father of the People's Republic of China from its establishment in 1949. It was erected forty years ago on the campus and had become a landmark of the university. Rufang was turned off. The square was not a romantic place at all for a date, but was only convenient for Su Yang because his laboratory was nearby.

While she was approaching the square, Rufang started to feel that it might just be wishful thinking on her part that Su Yang liked her, and what he wanted to talk about might have nothing to do with their relationship. She wondered why she had expected a proposal from him. She slowed down and breathed deeply to calm herself. She would never show her inner desire to a man. After all, Su Yang was not the Duke of Windsor, and why should she be infatuated with him?

It turned out that Su Yang did not propose to her. "Rufang, I have something to tell you," he said as they approached each other. "The Education Ministry is offering grants for two thousand PhD holders to do research abroad. Both of us are eligible for it, but we have to find a host university or institution. These are the materials of several American universities I collected online for you." A stack of loose pages were clipped neatly in a delicate case.

Rufang was disappointed because it was not what she had expected from Su Yang, but a gust of happiness swept through her, something that she had never experienced in her life. She persuaded herself that the kindness and consideration of the young man in front of her had not come from nowhere.

Sitting on the base stone of the statue, she flipped through the pages. It was hard to read those English-language materials because they were in small fonts and the green light from the bushes was too dim. She did it simply to show how grateful she was.

Su Yang came to sit down shoulder to shoulder with her, and she could smell the scent of the man. Her heart leapt and unconsciously she began to fan herself with the case in her hand on an already cold night. "A couple of young single women in my college have just run away," she told him. "And it says only married teachers are supported. It is an unwritten rule."

Su Yang answered with slight irony. "It's ridiculous! It's a prejudice in favor of the married."

Rufang shrugged helplessly. "What can we do about it? We're nobody and we can never decide our fate."

Su Yang turned to Rufang and then looked up at Mao Zedong as if he was seeking wisdom and strength from the former leader of the country. Then he patted her unexpectedly on the shoulder. "I've got an idea. Why don't you marry me? You won't be single then, and you'll have every reason to apply for the grant. This plan makes the best possible use of available resources to improve your living environment."

Rufang was too surprised to say anything. Her eyes were fixed on Su Yang, trying to read the expression on his face. Failing to decide if he was being serious, she felt as if she had been insulted. They were not boyfriend and girlfriend yet; how could he talk about marriage? If it was a trick to help her to get the grant, she would reject it and stay in China all her life.

Afraid of being misunderstood, Su Yang jumped to his feet and grabbed Rufang's arm.

"Rufang, we're no longer young undergraduate kids. We're old enough to free ourselves from those romantic notions. I like you. And I'm dying for a chance to go abroad with you. It took me years to speak my mind. You won't turn me down, will you?" Su Yang spoke with a slight stammer, but he carried it off without a hitch. He must have rehearsed his words many times.

It was what Rufang had longed for, although it was not as romantic and passionate as she had imagined. What was important was that he had proposed marriage to her, which filled her with happiness. However, she pretended to turn away in distain and threw the case with the collected pages of information about the universities abroad at Su Yang. "Students of sciences are notoriously stingy with money. Can several loose pages replace what is needed for a proposal?"

Su Yang suddenly realized that she had agreed to marry him and shouted almost hysterically. "No, they can't. They never can. I promise before Chairman Mao I will have an engagement ring made for Miss Xie, and I will kneel down to propose to you in a quiet place."

As a teacher of language, Rufang corrected Su Yang. "You're very out of date. People had rings made ages ago, but now they go to a jewelry shop to buy one. You're a postdoc, but you have problems with your verbs."

Su Yang returned the case of papers to Rufang. "If you'll be my language tutor I'll become a Chinese language expert in no time."

Rufang had never thought Su Yang was a person that was so quick to act. He asked her out for tea in the university's activity center for doctoral students. The tea house was rather empty and he put a small red velvet case on the table before her. Rufang was not unprepared for it, but she turned her head away shyly, pretending to enjoy her nice cup of green tea. It was not an occasion where she could act as if she could not wait to open the case. "You bring it back with you, but I have to kneel down to propose," Su Yang said.

Rufang could feel that her cheeks were burning with embarrassment, and she almost spat out the tea in her mouth. She winked at him. "Are you crazy? This is a public place and these people will be shocked."

Su Yang was only pretending to kneel down, so he sat down again to open the case. Inside the case was a small but delicate diamond ring. "It is a small one with a diamond of less than one karat, but it is genuine. I've had it tested in a laboratory in my department," Su Yang told Rufang.

Rufang put out her left hand, signaling Su Yang to put it on for her. At the moment she was deeply moved and a feeling of satisfaction came over her. As a postdoc, Su Yang was paid much less than a full-time researcher and he must have saved a long time for the small ring. What more can you expect from a man who willingly spends all that he owns on you?

It seemed the ring on her finger caught the eye of many living in the same apartment. Some of them were just curious and some appeared slightly surprised. "It is from my fiancé Su Yang, the postdoc in the School of Resources and Environment," she would simply answer when anyone attempted to fish for information about her boyfriend. She would say "thank you" instead of the indirect response typical of Chinese culture when she was congratulated. The university apartments for unmarried staff were in short supply, and the newly recruited teachers on the waiting list were expecting her to get married as soon as possible. She would have to move out when she got married.

The School of Languages had more female staff and several of them were well past the traditional age of marriage. These "left-over" PhD holders could not conceal their envy of Rufang and would nosily come to her office between classes, turning the room into a busy vegetable market. They were curious about how Rufang, who was quiet and a bit anti-sociable, could meet a postdoc in a completely different field without the knowledge of her colleagues. This was what Rufang was expecting. She was no longer single and she was going to apply for the research grant.

Rufang was rather surprised at how fast Su Yang was able to make contact with their target institutions. In about three weeks they received invitation letters from an American university and the host professors. With the letter from the A University in hand, Rufang had a strong urge to kiss the postdoc to show how grateful and excited she was. But she refrained from doing so.

"As resourceful as you are, how is it that you only met your first girlfriend after you obtained your doctoral degree?"

Su Yang was surprised, but he immediately recovered. "What if I ask you the same question?"

Rufang was calm. "That's not a good question. Good women outnumber good men in big cities. The shortage of good men has left women like me alone. Do you know what they say about the urban-rural difference in marriage? Women remain spinsters in cities, but many men stay single all their life."

Su Yang dropped his head, staring at his feet: "I came from a poor family in the country, and I had chosen to be single before I met you."

"But you bought this ring for me," she said, reaching out her left hand.

"It was my payment for working for my professor's state-supported environmental project. It was not enough for a bigger one." Su Yang was being perfectly honest.

What he said really touched her heart, and she moved over to kiss him long and hard. "It will be with me for the rest of my life," she said.

May 1, International Workers' Day, was a good chance for Rufang to go back home to Zhejiang with Su Yang to meet her parents, but she dismissed the idea. Back home, she would meet Caiqing and her other friends, and it would be embarrassing when they saw the small ring on her finger. Su Yang was a much better researcher than Caiqing's husband, who only knew how to make money by selling floor titles and paint. After all, she would never have Su Yang's doctoral degree framed to show guests, as Caiqing did with her son's passport.

## IV

As they had to pass an English proficiency test before they went abroad, Rufang and Su Yang registered for an intensive English class at the International Studies University. Away from their colleagues and students, the two found themselves among complete strangers, allowing them to relish their temporary newfound freedom. As a teacher of language, Rufang was better in English. Su Yang read English articles and books for his research project and he was never afraid of English tests, although his oral English was not as good. This allowed them to spend much of their time walking about the campus hand in hand, enjoying the romance of being alone.

It was drizzling the day they received their English test results, and the air was heavy with a mixed perfume of grass and flowers. "Rufang, why don't we get our marriage registration today?" Su Yang said as he looked out the window at the patchy rain. "Everything is done for the documents needed and we have to wait for the visas."

Marriage certificates had nothing to do with applications for passports and visas, but Rufang understood what Su Yang meant, because he had old-fashioned ideas about relationships and marriage and was against premarital sex. Rufang was somewhat disappointed, but she was more touched by his strong sense of responsibility towards her. It was then that she knew Su Yang would be her lifelong partner.

Coming out from the marriage registration office, they went to buy some chocolates to distribute among their colleagues, marking the beginning of their married life. They moved to an apartment for married staff. While Su Yang was busy filling out visa forms, making appointments with American visa officers, and trying to choose a cheaper flight, Rufang chose to stay at home preparing for something she considered part of her life in America: a baby with an American passport. She wanted to be the mom of an American child, just like her friend Caiqing, who was not as well-educated as her. She had never discussed this plan of hers with Su Yang, and she was not sure he would agree because he was an ambitious scientist and saw the chance to work in the U.S. as a rare opportunity for his academic career.

Rufang became pregnant as she expected. Excited as she was, she kept it a secret from her husband until the night before they went to the American consulate for their visa interview.

Su Yang was excited too, but his habit of rational thinking soon set him in a state of anxiety and confusion. "We're financed by state resources, but we're there to give birth to a baby. We won't be able to finish our programs," he said.

"Why are you always talking about programs and career?" Rufang replied. "We're given the opportunity, and our child can be an American child. Why do we give it up? Not everyone in China is so lucky, are they?"

Su Yang thought it was a ridiculous idea. "Why do you want a different nationality for our child? The Chinese economy is growing so fast. Can you imagine what China will be like in 20 years? When the child grows up, you may regret the decision."

Rufang thought of the framed passport of Caiqing's son, said: "If my child is American, I would have a green card and I can go to America anytime."

"You're a university teacher who is respected in China. What can you do in America? Be a housewife? That's why Professor Lu chose to come back. But his old classmate Zhong Kun has been jobless in America."

Rufang chose to be silent. She had to admit Su Yang was more rational and practical. It would be their first time alone in a foreign land, and the grant would only cover their tuition fees and basic living expenses. It would be quite costly to give birth in a hospital. They were not rich and could never afford what Caiqing's husband did for Caiqing when their son was born on the U.S. island territory.

Su Yang was even more worried about it. He believed it would be cheating F University as well as the American visa officers. They were not financially supported to go abroad to deliver a baby, and the American government would not give visas to those who only go there to give birth. It reminded him of a movie about a poor Mexican woman from the countryside who risked her life to cross the barbed wire along the U.S. border before her delivery. The baby was born an American citizen, as she wanted, but she was shot dead by an American border guard. Su Yang found himself breathing hard at the thought of the bloody scenes in the movie, making him upset at his wife's decision to obtain American nationality for their child at the considerable risk to her career and even her own life. It was an unwise decision he thought only uneducated village women would make.

In the following days, the couple was frantic with worries. As a competitive person, Rufang never changed her mind easily. She knew she had to face reality as the baby in her belly grew. Su Yang's best-laid plan for his research project, which was formulated with the help of his professor as part of his post-doctoral program, was about to be ruined. What he worried most was what would happen if the American visa officer discovered that his wife was pregnant in the interview. Her credibility would be destroyed and they would be refused visas to go to the U.S., and as a result, it would be difficult for them to go to any other country in the world in the future.

She tried to ease his mind. "I'll be only three month pregnant when we're interviewed. I'll have to wear a sloppy dress. Visa officers aren't obstetricians, and they would never know I'm pregnant."

"Then we have to keep it a secret between us. It's over if an email is sent to the consulate about it. They say pregnant women are sent back from American airports. Remember you have a J1 visa for a research scholar, not for a pregnant mother."

Rufang bought a dress with a flaring waist, which was longer than a shirt but shorter than a dress. It was the kind that teenagers would choose only because of its popularity. The style was post-modern to Rufang and she actually hated it. She wore it when she went out because it was tight at the chest and flared out to cover her growing belly.

The women in the college liked to talk about the clothes their colleagues wore. "Look, Miss Xie is going to America and she has switched to modernism," one of them said. But others were more unpleasant behind her back. "She's not a teenager anymore. Why is she acting so young?" Rufang was quite glad that she had succeeded in fooling them, because no one guessed the real reason why she chose the dress.

On the day of the visa interview, she matched the dress with a scarf, which was tied in a small bow on her chest, giving her that look of an active young woman with an air of shyness on her face. The visa officer in his fifties seemed quite happy and he smiled at Rufang while going over the documents. He finished the examination in no time. "You're newly married, so it'll be a perfect honeymoon for you," he said. She had never expected the interview to be that easy. When Su Yang finished his interview in the same window and they were out of the gate, they said they should have brought some wedding candies for the officer.

Rufang called the baby in her belly the "American guy." She started to learn on the Internet that American mothers are not confined to bed after childbirth and babies begin to learn how to swim even before they start to walk.

Su Yang laughed at her. "You really think our child is an American child?"

"Yes, it is," Rufang answered with a serious expression. "And we're the mom and dad of a real American guy."

"To be American is not that easy," Su Yang answered with a sigh. "We're paid about two thousand dollars a month. It is barely enough for our housing, food, and transportation. We don't have good medical insurance. How can we afford the expense of childbirth in America?"

Although Rufang shared her husband's worry about hospital expenses, it didn't dampen her excitement about having her baby in America. "Professor Lu has written Zhong Kun to tell him to help us when we're there. After all, it pays to have a child with a platinum passport."

Su Yang smiled bitterly. He did not want to

continue this debate with his wife, because mental stress would be damaging for a pregnant woman.

## V

Rufang and Su Yang took a China Eastern Airlines flight to the U.S. It was well past supper time, and all the passengers were in deep sleep under their blankets or with sleep masks. Rufang did not touch her supper, and the aircraft was encountering severe turbulence, making her feel terribly sick. Su Yang asked for a cup of hot water for her. "You've got to bear up when you want to be the mom of an American guy," he whispered in her ear. "It doesn't matter much if the flight attendants think you're pregnant. But you can never give yourself away before the custom officers at San Francisco Airport. It will undo all our efforts, you know."

Rufang nodded with a determined look on her face and then emptied her cup. "I'll be okay. I have plenty of plum candies. They help a lot."

Su Yang was obviously touched and clasped her to him, thinking it would have saved them the worry if she had not had the idea of giving birth to a baby in the U.S.

When the plane was approaching San Francisco, Rufang went to the toilet to wash up, trying to make herself into a different woman. She became so nervous at the customs counter that she had to put her hand on her chest to calm herself down. It was late at night and the black woman officer seemed sleepy due to her night shift. She took a quick glance at Rufang before stamping her passport. Rufang was rather surprised that it took her less than one minute to go through the process. Thinking about how easy it was at the visa interview, Rufang thought it was her destiny to be the mom of an American child.

Zhong Kun came in his Ford to meet the couple at the airport. It was an old model that was seldom seen in Shanghai. "It is twenty-five years old," Zhong Kun said when he saw Rufang look at his car. "I bought it when many Chinese people here could hardly afford a bicycle."

As she had met Zhong Kun and Professor Lu had written to him about their arrival before they left China, Rufang was rather frank. "Mr. Zhong, it works for me. But you have to use a better one when Professor Lu is here. He owns a Buick and he is picky about cars."

Zhong Kun laughed loudly when he noticed that Su Yang was patting Rufang's back to signal for her to stop talking about the car. "Of course, I will. Professors in China have fancy cars so they can look good in front of their students. You know, Americans began to use private vehicles more than a hundred years ago, and there are only some of them who would admire those who drive expensive cars." He meant he could afford a fancy car but he uses an old one, because a car had nothing to do with the social status of the owner.

With some effort, Rufang got into the car. Zhong Kun was a bit surprised when he caught a glimpse of her belly. He agreed to Professor Lu that he would rent a room in his apartment to the couple, but he never expected that they came to give birth to a baby. With a newborn baby in the house, his other tenants were sure to complain about the noise. He would lose money if they chose to move out or ask for a cut in the rent. As the couple had just arrived, Zhong Kun remained silent and drove the couple to their place. But when he got home he called Professor Lu immediately.

Zhong Kun's smile was sour when he thought of his old classmate Lu Jianhua's nickname and the scornful reaction of Rufang to his old car. "Old Lu, are you sure the lady is Su Yang's wife?" He asked knowingly when his friend answered on the other end of the line. "I have the feeling she is a mistress of yours. Many rich Chinese men are sending their mistresses to the States to give birth to babies. It saves them from troubles with their wives. I wondered why you tried so hard to find housing for this female student of yours."

The professor was quite upset with these words, but he lowered his voice due to the fact that his family was around him. "Nonsense. The two are newly married, and they are supported by the state to do research in the States. Why would they be there for a baby?"

Zhong Kun could sense how honest the professor was and then switched topic from jokes to business. "I see you are professor and student. You know, business is business. I agreed to a monthly rent of four hundred dollars, but now I have to charge them two hundred more. Four tenants share the apartment, and I am not sure they would continue to live there if they have a roommate with a noisy baby. The money serves as a security deposit."

The professor gave a derisive laugh. "That's your capitalist nature. You care more about money than loyalty to your fellow countrymen, don't you?"

Zhong Kun ignored the professor. "Let me tell you something else. I agreed to rent my room to your student and nothing more. You know, it's quite expensive to give birth to a child here in the States and they don't have medical insurance. Who knows what will happen to them?"

Professor Lu did not sleep well that night. He wondered why Rufang chose to have a baby in the U.S. instead of benefitting academically from the grant. In his eyes, she was an ambitious career woman. He could not persuade himself that she valued American nationality for her child the way those poorly educated Chinese women did.

The apartment was at least thirty years old, with four small rooms for four different tenants. The large living room had nothing but an old TV set with an eighteen inch screen, which gave out an impression of meanness. The couple was told the living room, the kitchen, and the bathroom were shared and had to be kept clean after each use. Rent was collected on the first day of every month, and that only cash payment was accepted. Bank checks were not allowed, probably to evade taxes. "Today is August the twenty-ninth," Zhong Kun had said to them. "I won't charge you for the next three days, because I'm a friend of Professor Lu. But I'll come on September the first." The landlord left in a hurry, leaving the couple alone and feeling lost.

Rufang had thought she could ask Zhong Kun about things like the nearest hospital, but she bit her tongue, thinking that would be too much trouble for the landlord. Luckily, a young roommate from Hong Kong, called Xiao Ding by the other roommates, offered to help. After immigrating to Canada as a skilled migrant, Xiao Ding worked as a programmer in Montreal with a handsome income. However, when the economy began to go into a recession, his small company was gobbled up and he was laid off along with the majority of his colleagues. He came to the U.S. to try his luck out in a computer company managed by a Chinese American, where he worked part-time. He was thirty-five and remained single. Xiao Ding was rather surprised to learn that Rufang was looking for a maternity hospital. "You're here to give birth to your baby? Do you have medical insurance? To my knowledge, the one for childbirth is as high as two hundred dollars a month. If you do not have it, you need to go to a public hospital. They don't charge, but you have to wait for a month or two."

"What do guys like you do? Does everyone pay that much for medical insurance?" Su Yang asked.

The young man smiled bitterly. "I can't afford it on my part-time salary, but I'm a Canadian citizen and I have my healthcare back in Canada. I go to a drugstore when I have a temperature or headache. I sometimes go to a Chinese doctor. If that doesn't work, I go back home. I simply can't afford American insurance."

Rufang realized that she had been wrong in thinking prenatal examinations were free as part of a national insurance system in welfare countries like the U.S. She felt uneasy, but she forced a smile to save Su Yang from worrying about her. "It doesn't really matter that much. I was thinking about going for a prenatal examination. I'm doing well. And the baby must be doing well, too. I actually don't need it."

"You're friends of the landlord. Why don't you go to a public hospital in his car?" Xiao Ding suggested. "You know, I can't afford a vehicle and I use the subway to go to work. I would help if I had a car."

The couple thanked the young man and went back to their room. Su Yang switched on his laptop to check his emails and among them was a message from Professor Lu. The Professor explained that Zhong Kun will charge more rent because the baby on the way might drive other renters away. After she finished reading the message, Rufang threw herself onto the bed as though she had fainted. She had prepared for the childbirth before she left China, but all she had in her Chinese bank was about five thousand U.S. dollars. They were no longer paid by their Chinese university and they had to pay their monthly share of the housing fund, endowment insurance, health insurance, and unemployment insurance. With a monthly grant payment of one thousand dollars for each of them, they could barely keep themselves above the poverty line in this country. That was why she was glad about being able to rent the cheaper room in the apartment with the help of her professor. She was upset that the rent had increased by half.

Su Yang tried to calm her down. "We're new here in a foreign country, and we can do nothing about it but accept the offer. When we're familiar with the surroundings, I'm sure I can find a part-time job to make some money. Believe me, I'll do it." However, Su Yang himself did not feel confident about being able to find a job, because he did not speak acceptable English and his research field would not help much. He did not want to be a dishwasher like the people of Professor Lu's generation did when they were in the U.S.

# VI

It was the morning of the first day of September, and Rufang found that all three renters were in the living room when she came out of her room, as if they were ordered to do so. Soon Zhong Kun came into the house, and the renters began to pay their rent one after another. The landlord looked around in each room to make sure that no damage had been done to it. He was a bit embarrassed when Rufang handed over her rent to him. "Rufang and Su Yang, Professor Lu must have told you about my decision. I wish you could see I was forced to do so," he told them. "I bought ten houses before the economic recession and I only manage to keep up my mortgage payments by renting out nine of them. But as the economy began to collapse, the rent levels kept falling and several of them were simply left empty. Eight of them were repossessed and this was the only one left for me to rent. You know I myself live in the other one. I depend on the rent for a living and I can't afford a cut in the rent."

"Mr. Zhong, we appreciated your help with our housing. It saved us the trouble of having to look for a place in a completely new country," Su Yang replied. "You know Rufang is pregnant and she has to go to a public hospital for a prenatal examination. The hospital is far away from where we live, but we don't have car. Can you help us when you have the time?" The couple had agreed it would be better if the extra rent was paid to the landlord in exchange for some help.

Knowing it had been unexpected and steep for the couple when he increased the rent at the last minute, Zhong Kun promise to help them. "No problem. I'll come over in a couple of days to take Rufang in my car to the hospital."

The small hospital was in a small city along the Warren Freeway. With several ambulances in front of the gate, it seemed to be a nice hospital to Rufang. Zhong Kun helped her with the registration, and a Chinese American nurse told her in a soft voice that a type-B ultrasonic inspection would be arranged for her in twenty days. Hearing she had to come again, Rufang was rather shocked. This type of examination was often done at a community hospital in Shanghai minutes after registration. She did not understand why she had to wait for weeks, and she was disappointed that they had come all this way only to fill out a form for the examination.

Zhong Kun smiled bitterly. "Rufang, this is the way they do things in public hospitals. It's totally different in a private hospital, but you need a fully comprehensive insurance."

Su Yang was quite upset. "What happens to a poor man who needs an emergency treatment? He just waits for his death in the long line?"

"The poor can't afford to be ill. To be healthy is everything for them," Zhong Kun answered.

Twenty days later, the landlord came again to take Rufang to the hospital. A woman obstetrician told Rufang that the fetus was not in a normal position in her uterus and suggested she be hospitalized for a manipulation of the fetus to help with the delivery. However, it could only be done in a private hospital.

A deep sense of despair overwhelmed Rufang and her face was convulsed with anxiety. "I'm new here in America," She tried to explain in English. "How can I afford it? I don't even have medical insurance."

"Ms. Xie, as an obstetrician, I do what I'm supposed to do. I'm sorry I can't help you with your problem. I'm sorry you have to leave now because the next patient is coming," the doctor answered in a gentle voice. It seemed the obstetrician had heard this story many times.

Rufang started to sob on her way home. Su Yang, who found the whole thing extremely perplexing, attempted to calm her down, but his words did not help much. Zhong Kun drove in silence, thinking he would be heaping up endless trouble for himself if he got involved. However, he would not ignore Professor Lu, who asked him to help his student. He then decided to stay out of it, defining his role with the couple as a purely business relationship between a landlord and his tenants. He would not ask for trouble for himself.

After Rufang fell asleep, Su Yang went downstairs to smoke, because smoking was not allowed inside the building. In addition to the baby on the way, he also worried about his program. He had been in the U.S. for nearly a month, and his professor and colleagues back home had asked about his plan several times, but he had not decided on the courses he was going to take. What would they think if they knew he had been busy preparing for a baby? He decided not to tell them the truth, but he did not know how to reply.

Xiao Ding came back late from work and saw Su Yang smoking downstairs with quite a number of cigarette ends scattered around him. "Mr. Su, you haven't gone to bed yet? We can't throw cigarette butts about. The meddlesome neighbors may report the landlord for it and we renters have to pay if Mr. Zhong has to pay a fine."

Su Yang collected the cigarette butts and told Xiao Ding about the examination results on their back to the apartment. The young programmer realized that Su Yang was asking for his help by telling him about his private matter. The warmhearted young man remembered that he had seen pregnant women from China at his company for appointments with his boss' wife. They talked about postpartum care centers and babysitting services. It seemed that the wife was engaged in the business. "Don't worry, Mr. Su. I'll ask my boss' wife tomorrow to see if she can help. We men have many hurdles to clear in our lives, and to get married and start a family is one of them. That's why I remain unmarried in my thirties."

Su Yang nodded with tears in his eyes and patted Xiao Ding on the shoulder passionately as an expression of his gratitude. However, for Su Yang, to get married is part of everyone's life and to have a new baby is a blessed event, which was celebrated with family and friends. More importantly, with the healthcare service in China, he would have been free from the worries that he was struggling with in America. He started to wonder, with a flashing feeling of resentment, how his wife had gotten the idea to give birth to a child of American nationality in a country across the Pacific, only to put them in a difficult situation even before the child was born. To save his own face, Su Yang would not tell Xiao Ding why his wife chose America as the birthplace for their child, but Xiao Ding already had an informed guess about it having been in Canada and the U.S. for years.

Xiao Ding went to see his boss' wife the next day. Before he finished telling her about the problems that Su Yang encountered, the lady asked him several questions. "What does her husband do for a living? Do they have enough money for it? What healthcare plan do they have?"

For a moment the questions left the young man at a loss for words, but he answered the first one honestly. "The two doctoral degree holders are from mainland China. They are supported by the state and they've been here only a couple of months."

"They're poor research assistants," she said with a mocking smile. "I thought they were a rich businessman and his mistress."

"The baby is in the wrong position, but they don't have the money for treatment in a private hospital. I'm here to see if we can help them. After all, they're Chinese too."

The lady didn't smile anymore and she began to list the items. "This is what my center charges for the services: three thousand a month before the birth of the baby, ten thousand for natural birth, two thousand a month for postpartum care, and another five thousand for the birth certificate and passport. You said the baby is in the wrong position, right? That'll cost much more before the birth of the child for measures to prevent miscarriage and additional services. They don't have the money, do they?"

"No, they don't," Xiao Ding answered softly, feeling embarrassed. "That's why I'm here for your help."

The mocking smile flickered across her face

again. "My business is for making money. I'm not doing it for charity. China has more than one thousand million people. If all Chinese women choose the U.S. as the birthplace for their babies, America would be another China. You see what I mean?"

As usual, Xiao Ding came back home late. He could imagine how disappointed the couple would be when he told them what the services would cost. When he entered the house, the couple was watching TV while waiting for him to come home. The old television with a small screen had poor picture and was seldom used by the other tenants.

Xiao Ding threw himself into the old sofa near Su Yang. He looked down at the floor for a while before speaking. "Mr. and Mrs. Su, I know you have been waiting for me. They have the services, but it costs at least twenty thousand dollars." He repeated the list of items and the couple was stunned into silence, making the muffled noises from the television even more harsh and unmusical.

# VII

Su Yang started to attend the two seminars he had chosen and worked in a laboratory. He would not have done it if he did not have to report what he was doing to his professor and colleagues back home. Rufang also registered for a couple of courses, but she had not shown up for the classes, staying at home all day for the safety of her baby. It was her first priority at the moment, except the short time spent shopping. Before coming to the U.S., Su Yang planned to visit the Grand Canyon and go sightseeing with friends on the weekends, but now he spent more time with Rufang, which made her feel sorry for him.

Across the hall in the same building lived a single Hispanic woman named Emma, who often had friends of different colors from her church coming over to stay with her. Emma spoke English with a heavy Spanish accent, and Rufang found it hard to understand her. "Rufang, why don't you come with me to church?" Emma asked one morning when she saw Rufang watching TV in the living room. "It's more fun than watching these dull

TV programs."

The church was not far from where they lived, and Rufang could see the chaste cross on the top of the building from her back window. Around the church was a large carefully tended lawn, on which people talked to one another in small groups after the services on Sunday. Rufang was not interested in religion, equating church goers with the pious worshippers at the Chinese temples. But she was curious about the church and thought it would be nice to practice her English with the people in the community. Rufang was a bit embarrassed. "I'm pregnant and the baby is in the wrong position. I'm afraid too much outdoor activity would be bad for it."

A young woman of Rufang's age, Emma patted Rufang on the cheek the way a mother did to her daughter. "Poor child, outdoor activities will only do you good when you deliver. Believe me, I was trained in a school of obstetrics to be a midwife and I now work as a head nurse in a private clinic."

Rufang was highly excited about it, and she had never expected that her Hispanic neighbor was a midwife, someone who is trained to help women give birth to babies. Thinking Emma would be a great help to her, Rufang rose and was ready to go with her to church, which made Su Yang worry. "Emma, do you think it is good for a pregnant woman to mix so much with other people?"

With her hands on her waist, Emma challenged him. "Mr. Su, do you think your wife will have an easy delivery if she spends most of her time watching TV? I can see you're a good father, but that's only after your baby is born. I know much more than you what your wife should do now."

Su Yang did not argue with Emma and he agreed by waving his hands in the air in an American manner. He felt much relieved when the two women went out and began to read the materials for his seminars. He had been blaming himself for wasting much of his time in the U.S. feeling sorry for his professor and fellow researchers, who expected him to introduce new areas of research to his university.

Rufang was warmly greeted at the gate of the church. Although she did not look pregnant yet, the manner in which her companion dealt with her made the crowd stand back and offer a longer bench to them. Several old ladies came over to introduce themselves and praised Emma for bringing a lost sheep to the Lord. Rufang understood what they were saying. It was out of curiosity that she came to church and she did think she would be a possible convert to any religion, but she would not tell them about it, especially when they were so kind to her.

An elegant middle-aged Chinese man was explaining a chapter in Luke on the platform. Emma told her that he was Mike Luo, the priest of the Chinese Evangelical Church in the community and that his wife ran a clinic for women, where Emma worked as a nurse.

Turning her head to the platform, Rufang felt she was lucky to join the group in the church. If she was introduced to Mr. Luo and then his wife, she would be given the opportunity for prenatal treatments, which, she hoped, might be free of charge.

After the services, Rufang chose to stand in front of the church, chatting with Emma. She went over to greet the priest as soon as she saw he was coming out, before Emma could be able to introduce her to him. "I'm glad you come to the church so soon after your arrival," The priest said with a smile. "Do you have believers in your family?"

Rufang's mother visited a temple in China at the beginning and in the middle of the month and she kept a statue of the Chinese Bodhisattva in their house. "Yes, my mother is," Rufang she answered.

The priest was pleased. "Mrs. Su, you and I are both Chinese, and we're both Christians, which means we're among the sisters and brothers. You're new here, so let me know when you need help. Our sisters and brothers help one another."

A deep sense of gratitude swept through Rufang and she could not help but to compare Mr. Luo and Zhong Kun, the two Chinese Americans. In no time Emma told the priest that Rufang had not had any prenatal treatment done due to her health insurance problem. "Why don't you come to my wife's clinic with Emma tomorrow for a check-up?" The priest said after a minute's reflection. "My wife had worked as an obstetrician in the well-known Margaret Williamson Hospital in Shanghai before we moved to America. I don't think she will charge for it."

While she nodded at the priest, Rufang felt tears were streaming down her checks. She felt the baby kick and it seemed it was pleased as well. At the moment, Rufang as an atheist thought she would rather choose to believe that God did exist, because it was Emma and Mr. Luo, both devout believers in Christianity, who offered to help when they were left helpless and alone in a foreign land.

Back home, when Rufang told him about the priest who offer to help, Su Yang was objectionable. "I'm a Party member, yet you mix with people in a church here."

Rufang curled up her lips with disapproval. "Our first priority at the moment is to make sure a healthy baby is born. Except for Emma and Mr. Luo, who else can we ask for help in this country?"

Su Yang chose to be silent. He was rational enough to know his wife was right that the Hispanic woman and Mrs. Luo's clinic were the only source of help for their baby. He knew he had to accept the reality.

Rufang came to the clinic with Emma. It was

a small cream colored building, with a brass plate reading "Jiang Meihui Obstetrics and Gynecology" in both Chinese and English. Jiang Meihui must be the name of Mrs. Luo, Rufang thought. The clinic was elaborately decorated. The waiting room had a floor-to-ceiling window with a white tulle curtain, which softened the sunlight. Waiting for her turn in the room, Rufang felt relaxed and peaceful, enjoying what she did not get in the public hospital.

Mrs. Luo came in. She reached out her hand while pulling off her mask. "Hi, I'm Jiang Meihui. You must be Mrs. Su. Emma and my husband have told me about you. Why don't we go upstairs for a type-B ultrasonic check? I need to learn about the position of the baby." The softly mellifluous voice with a forthright tone was typical of an experienced doctor, which helped Rufang to trust Jiang Meihui.

The results showed the baby in her belly was in a transverse lie, a position which would lead to a difficult labor if not corrected. "Mrs. Su, you have to be treated once a week, to help the baby to be in a vertical position before it is born," Jiang Meihui told Rufang. "You know, the baby has to get vertical to fit through the pelvis."

Rufang had not missed a word the obstetrician said, but she could not afford the payment for a weekly treatment. "We're new here, and we only have the basic health insurance. I'm afraid I can't afford it." Rufang felt embarrassed.

Jiang Meihui replied with a smile. "My husband and I converted to Christianity in America, but my clinic is not for charity, it's a business, you know. I know it's too costly for you, but I have a suggestion for you to consider."

Rufang looked up at the obstetrician with a hopeful expression on her face. "The two kids of mine were born here in America. They look Chinese, but they don't speak the language," Jiang Meihui said. "I thought about sending them back to China for a year to learn the language. When Emma told me you're a university teacher of Chinese, I got the idea for you to teach them the language two hours a week. It can be an exchange of your treatment at my clinic. Would that work for you?"

Rufang nodded repeatedly while Jiang Meihui spoke. "Thank you so much. That's a great idea. I'll do my best to teach them."

"Emma has agreed to give you a ride every time you come here. I think it's the best thing for you in your condition. The two kids will go to your place for their Chinese lessons on the weekends to save you the trouble of having you come to my home."

When Rufang was leaving for home, she felt the baby in her belly kick again. A gust of happiness swept through the mother-to-be.

## VIII

Luo Xiaodong and Luo Xiaoxi came to Rufang's apartment on time. They looked like the Chinese kids in Shanghai, but they spoke American English. Rufang had problems understating them when they spoke at the normal speed.

Rufang had been well-prepared for the lessons, and she was confident that with her help the two kids would be speaking Chinese soon. But the two found that it was not fun to learn the Romanization Pinyin system and the Chinese characters. Instead they asked questions about China. Does every Chinese kid go to McDonald's? Do they skateboard? Are they punished for addressing their parents by their names? Can they bring their toys to school and sell them to their fellow students? To the two American children, China was a remote country to which they were inextricably linked. They felt that they needed to know what happened, was happening, and will happen in the country of their parents.

Rufang answered the questions with infinite patience. She knew she had to be a teacher that they loved, because her work was done in exchange for her treatment in their mother's clinic. As soon as the questions were finished, she asked them to open their textbooks to start with the first lesson. Their homework was to talk to their parents at home in Chinese so they can make some progress.

By nature, Luo Xiaoxi, the girl, paid more attention to details than her brother. "Rufang, is Emma right when she said that you're here to give birth to a baby?" She asked, looking at Rufang's belly. "Why do you want to do it in America? It'll have to learn Chinese like what we're doing now. Doesn't seem like fun."

Not knowing whether to tell the truth to a

kid, Rufang's cheeks flushed red. Although she had never told Emma and the Luo's about it, it seemed it was an open secret, even to a kid like Luo Xiaoxi. "A baby is a gift from God, and no mother knows when it will come to her," Rufang said, reaching out to put the girl's cheeks in her hand. "I received it when I was in America. I didn't choose the time, did I?"

The metaphor amused Luo Xiaoxi. She laughed loudly, thinking Rufang was a nice teacher. They dutifully practiced the dull Pinyin and dialogues along with their teacher.

Later on, Rufang would prepare ice cream or snacks like potato chips for the two kids to help them to be more interested in their lessons. Once she forgot to do it, but still had the time to fry the several spring rolls that she bought from Chinatown and kept in her refrigerator. As soon as they opened the door, the aroma of the Chinese appetizers wafted towards them and they wanted to finish the food before starting the class. Rufang had small saucers for them and showed them how to dip it into the vinegar after each bite. When Luo Xiaoxi asked Rufang to eat the food, Rufang said that she had grown tired of spring rolls because she had too much of it in China. Actually, those were all that she had left, but she wanted the kids to have them. Rufang understood well that what she was doing for the kids was to please their parents so that she could receive the best treatment possible at the clinic. She was doing it for her baby.

Rufang met a pretty young lady every time she waited for her turn at the clinic. She was accompanied by another young woman in her twenties who helped her when she walked and took her bag for her in a manner which gave Rufang the impression that she was a hired helper rather than a sister. Rufang nodded at the two when they met but never spoke to them. Comparing their bellies, Rufang thought the young lady must have an earlier due date. One day when the helper was asked to fetch a bottle of water from the corner of the waiting room, she also got Rufang one. Rufang thanked the two women and started the first conversation between them. To Rufang's surprise, the young lady had a Zhejiang accent when she spoke. They were from the same province in China, which made them feel a sense of camaraderie for each other.

The young lady, Jin Xiaozhen, was twenty-four years of age. Learning that Rufang worked at a university in China, she began to address her as Professor Xie. Rufang immediately corrected her "I'm only a couple of years older. Why don't you call me 'Sister' in our own tradition?"

Jin was glad about the informal address. "Sister, you looked familiar the first time we met. How wonderful that we're from the same place. I've been here several months and I'm lonely to death. It's nice to know someone who speaks the same dialect!"

"Is your husband here with you? It looks like your due date is earlier. Isn't it better if he is with you?" Rufang asked.

Jin seemed slightly embarrassed, but she answered as if she did not mind about not having her husband there. "Giving birth to a baby is the business of a woman. How can a man help if he is around?"

It reminded Rufang of what Caiqin told her about some rich businessmen in China who send their mistresses to America for giving birth. It saves them the many problems of a double life, and the two women would be too far away to fight with each other. Rufang had the gut feeling that Jin was a mistress of someone because a Chinese woman as young as her seldom could afford the expense of giving birth in an American hospital.

Several days later, Jin called Rufang to have tea at her house, telling her that she could send a car to pick her up. Although Rufang registered for courses at the university, she never attended any of the classes, thinking it would be awkward for her to show up as a pregnant woman. She stayed at home, filling up the time with knitting for the baby, which she sometimes found boring. She accepted the invitation. After all, Su Yang would not come back home until it was dark since he transferred to C University not long ago.

It was the young woman helper whom Rufang met at the clinic that came to pick her up. Jin lived in an apartment building near Chinatown in San Francisco. From her balcony, Rufang could see the Gateway Arch with the green-tiled roofs and the well-known inscription of the four Chinese characters by the revolutionary Sun Yat-sen: "The

Whole World as One Community." The streets had all Chinese shops and restaurants, resembling a typical community in China. People who don't speak a single word of English would have no problem communicating here, Rufang thought.

It was a spacious apartment, as large as the four bedroom apartment where Rufang lived. The young woman who drove her to the apartment was Jin's personal assistant, and another woman in her fifties was hired to do the housework. It seemed that Jin lived a much easier life than Rufang.

Rufang and Jin sat in the living room, enjoying their Chinese tea and sunflower seeds. The other two women, who seemed to have been in the business long enough to know the informal rules well, were busy in the kitchen until they were called for their services. As a guest, Rufang sipped her tea slowly and cracked her seeds, waiting for the hostess to tell her about the purpose of the meeting.

"You told me to call you 'Sister' instead of 'Professor Xie,' and I will look on you as a friend," Jin said. "You must have guessed rightly. I am what they call a 'mistress' or 'the other woman.' The man was my boss. He's married with a daughter, who is now a university student. I found myself pregnant with his child, but he didn't want to divorce his wife. That's why I'm here as an investor immigrant. This apartment was a gift from him. It cost him seven hundred thousand dollars." While speaking, Jin looked up at the ceiling, smiling contentedly.

"He's not coming when you're in the hospital?" Rufang asked.

Jin smiled bitterly. "He's too busy with the several companies of his. Luckily, I get twenty thousand dollars every month from him. It's more than enough for the two helpers and my clinic expenses. He has promised to double it after the child is born. He'll buy me a large diamond ring, too. Even his wife doesn't have a diamond one." As she spoke, the bitter smile was gradually replaced by an expression of wistful juvenile longing.

"What are you going do after the child is born? Go back to China?" Rufang tried to keep up the conversation.

"I'm an immigrant, and my child will be American by birth. We'll naturally have the social benefits that an American enjoys. Why do we want to go back home? What's more, the old hag claimed

she would disfigure me by hurling acid at my face."
Jin waved her hand at Rufang when she spoke, as if
it was Rufang who would be sending her back to
China.

Jin was surprisingly quick with picking at her
sunflower seeds. When she saw the heap of seed
shells before her, she told the housemaid to clear
the tea table and prepare some Ningbo-style soup
balls for the two of them. "Sister, why don't stay in
America after your childbirth?" Jin asked Rufang, as
they sat down at the table for their meal. "Your child
will be American and you as the mother can renew
your visa. And you can apply for a green card later."

"I'm not as lucky as you to have twenty thous-
and dollars to burn every month," Rufang replied.
"My husband and I are supported by the government for our continuing education programs,
and we are paid only one thousand dollars each
a month. Our life here is much harder than it
was back home." Rufang felt a twinge of envy at
the thought of Jin's life, who lived in a spacious
apartment with two helpers. Jin had the best health
insurance and she was free from the trouble that
Rufang had about giving birth.

Jin smiled at Rufang. "Sister, I wanted you to have a look of my apartment. If you think it is okay, you and your husband can mover over here to live with me. I have guest rooms and I won't charge you. I think you're well-educated people and I'll learn a lot from you if you're here with me. I'll become a total airhead if I only have the helpers with me all day long."

Not until now did Rufang see why she was invited. She was almost convinced, thinking they would save six hundred dollars if they moved. Back at home, she filled her husband in on the details about what she saw and heard about the mistress, hardly concealing her envy of the young lady.

Su Yang was rather surprised at her tone of voice. "Rufang, you have a PhD and you work for a university. Are you jealous of someone who is kept as a mistress by a married man?"

# IX

Su Yang was at a grocery store, struggling for a long time trying to decide whether to buy a chicken. As it was harder for his wife to move freely, he had to take over the work of shopping for the family. Su Yang learned from his mother that chicken soup was the best choice of food for pregnant women, so he suggested that Rufang cook it every day for herself. Chicken was among the cheapest meats at the grocery stores and Rufang was so tired of the soup that the smell would make her want to vomit. The chickens in America were kept in factory farms and the meat was tough and less tasty than free-range chicken. The chicken soup seemed tasteless to Rufang.

She loved prawn and salmon, but she knew Su Yang would never buy them. Seafood products were much more expensive in America and they had never tried any of them. They could not afford them even if they spent on food all the money left after they paid for housing, transportation, and other daily necessities. They had never eaten out in a restaurant. Rufang was not a good cook, but she was not a picky eater, either. She enjoyed whatever she had on the table, but now she had to think about the nutritional value of what she ate for the health of the baby in her belly. It was the responsibility of the mother to make sure that a healthy child is born. "Jin told me organ meat is available in some of the Chinese stores in Chinatown. Americans don't eat them, but we Chinese do. Why don't you pick up some the next time you're there? They're cheap."

Su Yang nodded. He felt sorry for his wife and the baby on the way that he had to search for cheaper things in grocery stores for the family, being unable to afford the food that she loved. At the same time he thought they would not have to live the life that they were living if his wife had not had the idea to give birth to the baby in America. That explains why she is jealous of Jin, the mistress of a rich businessman, he told himself.

Jin called Rufang often to chat or to invite her for soup at her home. Jin was recently introduced to the owner of Kan's Restaurant in Chinatown and she was so crazy about the signature soups by one of the chefs at the restaurant that she had the various nutritional soups delivered to her apartment. Of course, she could have any food sent to her because she had a baby in her belly and its father gave her money to burn.

Although Jin was simply being kind to her by inviting her for soup, Rufang began to make up excuses to not go. She realized that her husband was right and it would be beneath her as a university teacher with a doctoral degree to take advantage of the generosity of a mistress of a married man.

However, she had to watch every penny to make ends meet. Their monthly expenses had to be kept within the two thousand dollars that they were paid, and the money they brought with them had to be saved for baby expenses. When she passed a baby store, she would sometimes go in to look at the soft baby clothes, cradles with music players, and even diapers, which would fill her with feelings of excitement and happiness. She had not bought anything for the baby yet, because they were frighteningly expensive. Every time in the store, she would tell herself it would be a waste of money to buy those things that were made in China but sold in America.

Jiang Meihui came from China and she understood the problems Rufang faced. "Over the years numerous babies have been born at my clinic, and I'm still in contact with many of the parents," she told Rufang. "It would be a waste for them to throw away things they have only used a few times. I can ask some of them for those baby things for you if you don't mind."

Rufang was more than pleased. "Thank you so much. It's so nice of you. I don't mind at all."

In the following days, some clean baby clothes, toys, and a folding crib were brought to Rufang in Emma's car. The mother-to-be sorted those used baby things and placed them neatly in a corner of the room, which would be a place for the child, because she could not afford a special room for the baby as Jin did. Before going to be bed, Rufang would touch the toys and the crib and speak to her baby. Later, Su Yang joined the game, too.

Jin gave birth to a baby boy. She had her driver deliver red happiness candy to her friends and acquaintances. The candy were made of chocolate and wrapped in red paper with gilt lettering, meaning both festivity and prosperity. Rufang received a box containing twelve candies and she shared them with Xiao Ding and Emma. To Rufang's surprise, Emma frowned at the candy. "You Chinese distribute candy when you have a new baby in the family. I have candy almost every day in my office and I'm tired of them. Why don't you bring a hamburger to me?"

In the box was also a beautiful invitation card. The father of the baby, who was overjoyed that a boy was born to his family, was flying to San Francisco for a formal party to celebrate his first full month, according to Chinese tradition. The guests were to be hosted at Kan's Restaurant and Rufang and her husband were invited. Rufang started to worry about it, because a first month gift or a red packet with cash in it had to be prepared for the newborn, which would be an additional expense for her. If Jin had not held the formal party, they would send them happiness candy in return when their baby was born.

After dinner, Rufang brought the invitation to Su Yang, who dipped into his pocket after a brief silence and took out a one hundred bill. "This is for the gift. To start a family is a great event for a woman. We're invited, and we should follow the rules of the game."

Rufang was surprised at the unexpected cash, because it was she who managed the family income and her husband only had the pocket money for things like transportation. Su Yang then explained about the money. "To tell you the truth, I didn't go to my laboratory the past few weekends. I joined Zhong Kun on Bay Farm Island as a 'fishing guide.' We helped them with things like locating fishing spots and this is the money they paid me. I was a fishing champion when I was a teenager in my village. You do what I tell you, and you'll have a good catch. You're still wearing your regular dresses, and I actually intended to buy some beautiful maternity clothes for you."

Tears welled up in her eyes. "Su Yang, it was all about the child and me. I'm sorry you were forced to be a fishing guide when you preferred working in your laboratory."

Su Yang put on an air of nonchalance. "Don't fuss. I like fishing. I went fishing and I was paid. Why not to do it? After all, my Chinese colleagues are thousands of miles away. It's something between you and me."

But Rufang was worried. "What if Zhong Kun mentions it to my professor? It'll make us the laughing stock of the whole university."

Su Yang replied with a laugh. "He would never do that. He would lose his face if Professor Lu learned that he is making a living by renting this apartment and working as a fishing guide, after more than twenty years in America."

Putting the bill into her purse, Rufang could feel the warmth of her husband on it. She went over to sit shoulder to shoulder with him. "Can you feel our baby kick? That's its way of saying thank you." He placed his ear on her bare belly and smiled contentedly.

# X

Seeing the swollen face and ankles of Rufang on the way to the clinic, Emma suggested she be hospitalized at Jiang Meihui Obstetrics and Gynecology before the birth of the baby. Rufang smiled her thanks but said she would choose not to do so. She would ask Jiang Meihui for nothing more than teaching her kids Chinese in exchange for her treatment. Emma made her suggestion from the point of view a professional nurse, but she did not know much about the interpersonal relationships between Chinese people. Jiang Meihui was the owner of the clinic where Emma worked as a nurse, and it was Jiang Meihui who decided whether Rufang should be hospitalized or not.

Rufang became worried, too, as her pregnancy progressed. Her young colleagues back home would ask for a maternity leave several months before the date of their childbirth, staying at home or in a hospital to avoid being spotted with a large belly. They would go back to work only when they resumed their shape. Rufang would have enjoyed the same right if she were in China. But she was in a different country—and she was not Jin, who was kept by a rich man. She felt she had been lucky enough to be given the free treatment at the clinic and it was impossible for her to ask for more.

When she was alone in the room, she would touch her large belly and speak to the baby. "My dear, you're here with Mom in a foreign land so that you'll be a citizen of the most advanced nation in the world. People will be jealous of your nationality wherever you go. As you grow up, you will not be pushed hard at school and you don't have to elbow your way into college. You'll live an easy life with the benefits from the government. When you reach eighteen, Mom and Dad can apply for our green cards. We'll be a happy and wealthy family." It seemed these words were spoken more for herself than for the child. She had to repeat those dreams of hers again and again, so that she could recover from the disappointment she had been experiencing in America.

Su Yang got up quite early in the morning to get a ride in the used car that Xiao Ding bought recently. Rufang felt sad at the thought that her husband did so, at the cost of a better sleep, to save the money for his subway travel, but she could not help in any way. Ever since they came to San Francisco, they had been in the habit of considering the cost before actions were taken. They had been saving every penny that could be saved for the baby on the way.

When she was alone in the living room during the day, she would knit while watching TV. Professor Lu emailed her several times asking whether she was writing research articles and, instead of telling him the truth, she told him that she had to learn about the current research methodology used in the American academic field before she started to write her own articles. However, one thing she was glad about was that she understood English much better with the television on most of the time.

She was watching the popular grey-haired anchorman's commentary on President Obama's plan for medicare reform when the CNN program was interrupted for a news flash. The live breaking news was about a school shooting that took place twenty minutes ago on the campus of C University, which resulted in at least a total casualty of a dozen victims.

Rufang's heart skipped a beat. Putting aside her knitting, she immediately called her husband, but his favorite ringtone, *Ode An die Freude*, was heard in the bedroom. Su Yang left his cell phone on the bed when he left in a hurry. She wanted to call his laboratory number, but remembered she had not jotted it down when he told it to her. She had ignored too many things in life due to her deep concern about the baby in her belly. Of all a sudden, she grabbed her bag and headed to the nearby subway station for C University. Too much in a hurry, she forgot she was pregnant and broke into a trot. She prayed to God again and again for the safety of her husband, the father of her baby.

Su Yang had left the campus to join Zhong Kun as fishing guides for a fishing contest for retired people on Bay Farm Island. Those were wealthy people and the two were expecting a handsome payment. Su Yang had no idea of what was happening on the campus and he had no access to television news on their way to the island.

It was the first time that Rufang took the subway. Hurrying along a long dim tunnel in the rapid transit center, she could feel the wind against her and going into the neck of coat. Realizing that someone was standing in her way, she looked up to find two men wearing dark down coats and woolly beanies, which covered most of their face. "I'm a pregnant woman!" She was so frightened that she shouted in a trembling voice, pressing her bag instinctively to her breast.

One of the men snatched the bag from her and the other punched her in the face and pushed her down into a dimmer corner before she could shout a second time. It all happened in less than a minute before the men vanished. A janitor called 911 when he saw the woman lying in a pool of blood. She was sent to a nearby hospital. She had to have an emergency C-section to avoid a massive hemorrhage, which had put the lives of her and the baby in danger.

When Rufang was rushed into the operating room, the police officers were already calling Jiang Meihui's office after a quick search of her cell phone contacts. When the obstetrician and the nurse arrived, the lovely child had been born, a baby girl to whom they had been given much attention to. Knowing that damage had probably been done to the baby as a result of the mother's injuries and the premature delivery, Jiang Meihui and Emma wept silent tears, wondering how Rufang would react to the news when she woke up from the anesthesia and how they could help her and the baby.

It was the third day since Rufang was admitted to hospital and she was still separated from her baby, who had been kept in an infant incubator under close observation in the intensive-care unit. As an American citizen, the child was treated free of charge at the hospital, but Rufang's basic health plan did not help her to pay the medical bills. She had to follow Jiang Meihui's suggestion to move to the obstetrician's clinic to avoid the astronomical bills.

With the help of Zhong Kun, Su Yang went to a social security office and it took him only half an hour to get a social security card for his daughter, which was needed for her passport.

The baby, who was named Su Chinamerica (Su Zhongmei) by the couple, was released from the hospital when she was exactly thirty days old, but was diagnosed with congenital moderate cerebral palsy with head and neck paralysis. The mother's tears brimmed over and fell on the brand new passport. She did not know whether it was a natural catastrophe or an act of God. The Lord may take from you when He gives and that's why there's no perfect life, she thought.

Zhong Kun and their roommates joined to celebrate the newborn's first full month. Xiao Ding helped to decorate the living room with little colored lights, which blinked on and off, giving the room an air of mystery. Emma came with a homemade cake with a red candle on the top, and

Zhong Kun offered to buy a crate of beer and a braised chicken. It was the first time that Zhong Kun was being generous since they first met in San Francisco.

Wrapped in a red silk coat, the baby was quiet as if she were not yet born. The adults enjoyed themselves in a somewhat gloomy atmosphere. The three men drank one toast after another, and the women nudged each other into having more of the cake.

Emma tried to console the young mother. "It's unfortunate to have a handicapped child in the family, but is not the end of the world. As an American citizen, Chinamerica is entitled to the excellent medical treatment here in America and it is free. Things will change for the better as she grows. And you yourself can apply for a Green Card."

Zhong Kun did not think it was wise to stay in America only for the sake of the child. "Su Yang and Rufang, never give up your teaching jobs in China for anything. Su Yang is doing science and it's easier for him to find a job. Rufang is in the field of arts and humanities, and to find a decent job is almost impossible for foreigners. You'll end up as a jobless guy with an American passport or a Green Card but living on unemployment money, just like me." Zhong Kun had drunk too much and he suddenly burst into tears. His tenants were rather shocked at the story of his own life in America.

# XI

Ever since their daughter was born, Rufang and Su Yang had been trying to decide whether to go back to China. Su Yang believed that it was shortsighted to stay in the U.S. just for the free medical care for their daughter. With a doctoral degree in the field to which he determined to devote himself, he would have a promising career in China. More importantly, he did not want to be another Zhong Kun.

Xie Rufang understood she could no longer put any pressure on Su Yang, who had sacrificed everything for their daughter. If Su Yang went back to China, she and her daughter had to get by on the government benefits for the child. She was not Jin, the mistress who did not have to work for a living. She believed that Zhong Kun was right when he talked about the difficulties that foreigners who had degrees in arts and humanities had to deal with in job hunting in America. She was trained as a Chinese language teacher, but numerous Chinese in San Francisco, whatever their native dialects were, seemed to be able to teach the language, so long as they were able to read the basic Chinese words. Among them, she was not competitive at all. In addition, she had never imagined a life with her husband living on the other side of the vast Pacific. Being tolerant and responsible, Su Yang had been serving the function of a shelter for her and her daughter in this foreign land, something she could never afford to lose.

The couple was in the Consulate General of China in San Francisco to obtain a visa for their child. As an American citizen, she needed a visa to visit her parents' country like other American people do.

Hearing about the disability of the child, a friendly middle-aged officer jotted down a telephone number while handing over the passport to them. "This is the phone number of an expert in congenital cerebral palsy in the Children's Hospital of Shanghai. He's a relative of mine, and I think he will be glad to help you."

It began to rain when they left the consulate. Rufang unwound her scarf for her baby when she found her smiling at her. She was so excited that she shouted at her husband, "Look, she's smiling for the first time!"

# Auschwitz Wall of Death

# 1

At long last I was about to book my summer holiday, after working for three whole years as a foreign correspondent. With a tourist map of Europe before me, I felt as if I were out in a garden and the seasonal flowers of city names were swaying in the May sunshine. I lightly passed my fingers over Rome, Barcelona, Geneva, Vienna, Prague, and Amsterdam ... They had been holiday destinations of my dreams, but now none of them was as tempting to me as the place I had already decided on.

I had read this book when I was a child and several lines from it have imprinted on my mind. "It was spring. A group of children was crossing a vast field hand in hand. None of them knew where they were heading. The girls picked wild flowers and waved them before the boys in a challenging manner. They giggled when the boys ingratiated themselves by offering their own flowers. In the eyes of the children were only flowers scattered in the field and they were still to learn about what was going on beyond it. It was only half an hour before the children and the flowers in their hands turned into a pall of black smoke that curled upwards into the sullen sky."

I was based in Lyon, France. Along the Tours Boulevard in the downtown of the city were tourist agencies. I went to one called Fajardo Farm, which I often visit for my air tickets to different places. I knew quite a few of the female staff there. Anne seemed excited when she saw me. "I knew you would come, Miss Journalist. The holiday is around the corner. Who wouldn't love sunbathing at the beach in this lovely weather? To spend a holiday in Lyon is too cruel to yourself, don't you think?" It seemed she had been waiting for me for years.

"How are you, Anne," I said, looking at her smiling face. "I'd like a ticket to Kraków, the southern city in Poland."

"Kraków, the old city? That's a lovely idea. Since you're going to Poland, I would suggest you visit Warsaw and Gdańsk as well." While she was speaking to me, she had already started checking the availability of the ticket on her computer, her eyes moving like radars.

"You're right, but I'm going to only one place in Poland. You see, it's here." I spread out a map of Europe and pointed to a red circle to the west of Kraków.

"Auschwitz?" Anne almost screamed. She shook her head and then stared at me for quite a long time, probably to make sure that I was not joking.

"Yes. I'm going to Auschwitz. I've been thinking about it for years, and I will go there this summer," I explained.

I knew several of Anne's colleagues were peeking in my direction. Like Anne, they must be puzzled that a young woman would chose a living hell for her summer holiday over enjoying the feel of the summer sun. Luckily, they knew I was a journalist, not an ordinary traveler who was trying to decide on a holiday destination.

The travel route Anne suggested for me was both economical and practical: I would fly with Lufthansa from Lyon to Warsaw via München.

Anne spent her honeymoon in Warsaw twenty
years before, so she suggested I include the city in
my plan. Then I could go on by train to Kraków,
which is near Auschwitz. What's more, I could go
back to Lyon from Kraków via München. Anne
handed me my travel itinerary. "Please come see me
when you are back and tell me about your holiday."
I agreed.

I noticed a young man sitting on the sofa
behind me, waiting to be served. He had slightly
curly black hair, with the sideburns forming two
natural crooks at the temples. His eyes were brown
and he had a happy face with a ready smile. He must
be a meek, good-tempered guy, I thought. In no
time, his face broadened into a smile at me. "Have
a nice trip, Miss," he said, holding out his hand
toward me, an act that somewhat surprised me. His
well-trimmed fingernails won my favor and I shook
his hand in spite of myself, while thanking him.

Sitting in a terminal hall at Lyon Satolas
Airport, I could see through the window my plane
on the parking apron outside the window, with its
logo of an encircled dark blue crane in flight.

"Hello Miss." It was the man I met at the

tourist agency. "How nice we meet again. Is this seat taken?" He stood in front of me smiling.

I was surprised to see him again. "No, it's not. You can take it." I motioned him to take the seat. "Are you going to München too?"

"Yes," he said with a big smile. "I'm going to Auschwitz to be exact, the place where you're going."

"Really?" I had the feeling that it was a concocted scheme. "We're going to the same place?"

"I learned at the tourist agency your destination was Auschwitz, and I thought that was a sign for me from God. Then I booked the same flight and the same hotel." He continued by introducing himself. "Joshua, engine designer, Jewish French."

"My name is Yao Yao, Chinese journalist." We shook hands for a second time.

I turned to the electronic screen, on which the rotating flight schedules were displayed. "Do you think forty minutes is enough for us to transfer at München?" I asked.

"Germans are incredibly obsessive about punctuality." Joshua answered with a smile.

We spoke no more, nor did we talk about

Auschwitz, our destination. Both of us knew to visit the notorious death camp in a summer holiday was more than a pleasant trip.

Quite a number of German-speaking passengers gathered before the departure gate. They must work in France and were on their way back home to spend their holidays. I called my family in Shanghai to tell them about my trip to Poland. When I finished, a German lady asked me in English in an excited voice, "Miss, are you from Shanghai?" A German lady asked me excitedly in English when I finished my phone call.

"How did you know?" I asked, nodding.

"It sounded like you were speaking Shanghainese on the phone. I don't understand it, but I'm familiar with the accent. We have been in Shanghai for five years, living in the new district of Gubei. We're on our way back for our holiday."

Her husband and son smiled at me. "*Nong hao*," the son plucked up enough courage to greet me with a "hello" in Shanghainese.

My house was about a quarter of a mile drive from where they live. I smiled and told them that this was a small world. "We may meet on the streets someday," her husband added.

Lufthansa is my favorite airline. Upon entering the cabin, passengers were lapped in culture. J. S. Bach piano concertos were played, and the walls were decorated with small oval frames in which are ingenious quotes from Johann Christoph Friedrich von Schiller and Johann Wolfgang Von Goethe. People spoke in tiny voices and even kids were careful when peeling their fruits or removing candy wrappers so that they did not disturb their neighbors. Seeing all this, I began to wonder what forced a people with so much emphasis on education and non-material culture to establish the concentration camps? I didn't know what Joshua thought about it, but I wouldn't discuss the question with him on the plane, which might offend the neighboring German travelers.

The München Flanz Josef Stlauss International Airport is an enormous airport with numerous transfer tunnels. The sign at each entrance was so helpful that travelers who didn't speak the language would have no trouble finding their way. It took us less than ten minutes to get to the gate for our flight to Warsaw, and we still had time to enjoy a cup of free coffee.

"Everyone admires Germans for their punctuality. It was reported that Nazi soldiers were never late for their concert after they shot millions of kids and their parents," Joshua said in French. His voice was so low that it seemed he was murmuring to himself. Still, he looked around in fear that the neighboring Germans, who had fine-tuned ears, could understand what we were saying in French.

What Joshua said made it even harder for me to understand why such a highly civilized people with many musicians and philosophers in their history could have ever thought of creating the Auschwitz camp. This question had puzzled me for years. I had read many books and watched films about it, but I won't believe it until I saw it myself.

## 2

Anne suggested we stay for three days at Hotel Ibis in Warsaw. She must have thought we needed enough time to prepare ourselves before we go to Auschwitz.

Compared with the München Airport, Frederic Chopin International Airport in Warsaw was pale and old, and all the concrete buildings were block-shaped that reminded me of a face with a deadpan expression. As neither Joshua nor I had been to Poland before, we looked, as a conditioned response, for instructions in a language we could understand, but it was in vain. All written words in the airport were in Polish. We had no choice but to follow the crowd with our creaking carts.

"What language do you speak besides English and French?" Joshua asked.

"Chinese, of course," I answered him. "What about you?"

He laughed bitterly, "Hebrew."

Like beggars pushed against the wall, we hopelessly searched for signs we could recognize. As a sharp-eyed woman, I saw a big "I" on the roof a small block-shaped pavilion outside the gate of the airport.

"Information," I shouted, my heart leaping with joy, as anyone who is unexpectedly rescued from a desperate situation would feel.

The woman at the information desk was

very young, probably fresh from college. When asked if she could speak English, she nodded with hesitation, but I could sense a touch of nervousness on her face. I gave her the hotel address through the window and asked how we could get there. She answered in her broken English with the help of hand gestures. I tried to figure out what the body language meant and Joshua made sentences with her English words. At last, we understood that we could take number seventy-four bus to the downtown area where we could walk to our hotel.

We heaved a sigh of relief. Although there was only one route for the subway, the buses went everywhere in the city. The number seventy-four bus looked rather old, like the ones I saw in Shanghai when I was a little girl. Tickets were handled by the driver instead of a conductor, so passengers went on board from the front. To cross the language barrier, we had some euro coins in our palms, so that the driver could pick up whatever the tickets' worth. But it seemed he was rather upset, complaining loudly in Polish. I suddenly realized that Poland was still not using the euro even though it was already an EU member. The driver was actually sharp-tongued but tender-hearted. Seeing I was quite embarrassed, he waved his hand, which meant I could take his bus without paying. But he was not so nice to Joshua and took a two-euro coin from his hand, probably because Joshua looked more like a European guy, who he thought should not cadge a free ride.

The creaky bus went slowly along for about twenty minutes before the driver turned to shout "Hi," motioning with his hand that it was the place for us to get off. This must be the downtown area. The street was about eight-lane wide with a very busy crossroad. There were several tramcar rails along the street and between the rails and the asphalt road grew wild bushes more than one foot tall. Part of the bushes were heavily trafficked by pedestrians, but new grass was visible on the ground. As there was no pedestrian overpass or underground tunnel along the wide street, Joshua and I looked at each other and shouted "one, two, three" before we ran to the other side of the street, as if we were crossing an enemy line on a battle field.

While the young woman at the information desk told us we could walk to our hotel when we get off the bus, I tried to make sure that we were taking the right way by asking about the hotel. I picked young people on the street because they tend to speak more English than senior citizens. Every answer helped to bring us closer to the hotel.

"Hotel Ibis? It's not too far away. Just go straight ahead."

"You mean the hotel? It's just around the corner."

A girl told us it was just "under your nose." But it took us more than twenty minutes to get to the hotel since we left her. Of course, I gained a much better understanding about what Warsaw people meant by "walking distance"; it was four kilometers from the bus stop to the hotel. When we arrived at the hotel, nearly an hour had passed.

The logo of Ibis with its red flowers in a green background exuded a feeling of warmth and welcome. The girl at the check-in counter spoke natural English and her charming smile blew away our weariness from the trip. I was given a room on the fifth floor and Joshua was given one on the sixth. We agreed to meet in the lobby and then go to a Chinese restaurant for dinner.

"You are lucky. Orange Red is just within walking distance. They offer the best Chinese food in town," the young woman at the lobby counter said, while carefully drawing a circle on my map. To our surprise, we got to the restaurant forty-five minutes later by asking a couple of people on the way.

The owner of the restaurant was from Hebei Province in China. "This is Warsaw," he said with a bitter smile as he listened to our stories. "You can only believe half of what they tell you and the other half is probably not true."

I explained to Joshua what the restaurant owner said and he responded with a smile. "This city was a victim of many disasters. Strangers would forgive her for anything if they knew how much she suffered."

The owner of the restaurant made Chinese greens for us. Joshua fondled the exquisite tea cup while enjoying his tea. Suddenly, he raised his head. "Yao Yao, you're a journalist. Don't you want to know why I'm visiting Auschwitz?" He asked. "Are all Chinese people as reserved as you?"

"You haven't asked me the same question

either. You are my traveling partner. You are not being interviewed. Is it right to ask about your purpose?" It sounded as if I was not interested at all, but actually for numerous times I had stifled my curiosity about his trip. To keep his interest on the topic, I told him my purpose was to make myself believe the death camp was not imaginary but real.

Our order—fried rice with egg, fried spring rolls, and sweet and sour soup—was served. The authentic Chinese food gave an edge to our appetite, so much so that we had to delay the discussion about the concentration camp. In no time we cleared the food on the table and another pot of tea was served. "Yao Yao, you journalists travel a lot and are better informed than us. Do you know the organization called 'Operation: Last Chance'?"

I shook my head. "I work as a volunteer for the organization," Joshua said.

While more than six decades had passed since the end of the Second World War, hundreds of Nazi war criminals still hide in different parts of the world, most of them nearing the end of their lifetimes. No one would know who they are when they pass by. Time is a magician that heals wounds from which blood flowed heavily, and even criminals believed it has cleansed the blood from their hands. However, historian Efraim Zuroff, the overseer of the organization, holds a different opinion. Their mission is to track down ex-Nazis still in hiding and bring them to justice before they die.

Joshua told me that Zuroff had a list of the most wanted Nazis who are still alive and manages to identify them. Two years before, when people were filing out of a synagogue in Budapest, he announced at a press conference that a Nazi war criminal that sent one thousand two hundred Jews to their deaths in 1942 lived in an apartment opposite the synagogue. Joshua was visiting the synagogue, and he became a friend of Zuroff's and a member of the organization.

Joshua is my age, but I knew that he as a Jew feels much more pain than I do when that part of history was scrutinized. "Does your trip have to do with the organization?" I asked him. He shook his head. "No war criminal is so stupid that he lives in Auschwitz. I'm looking for Yura, the sister of my grandmother, who I have never met before. Seventeen members of my grandparents' families were killed between 1939 and 1945. Yura is the only one whose whereabouts haven't been confirmed. Auschwitz may be the last place where I can find her whereabouts."

Joshua took out a black and white photo from his wallet. Clearly, it was a reproduced one. In the photo a young woman leaned against a tall tree. She had permed curly hair, a lacy shirt, a gingham skirt, and a pair of sandals with holes in them. She had long, slender shapely legs. Her sweet, warm smile was an indicator of the happy life that she led. That was Yura, who, I could see, was from a well-to-do family. She was taken away by Geheime Staatspolizei from her house in Strasbourg in the winter of 1941 and there had been no news about her ever since. She stared at me, as if telling me that she was expecting Joshua and me.

I had no idea how long we stayed in the restaurant, but I remembered that our tea pot was refilled again and again and that we were the last to leave. We left more than enough tip for the owner of the restaurant.

# 3

The city of Warsaw is simply a riddle for an outsider, to which no one knows the answer. Poland had already joined the EU and opened its borders to its neighboring nations, but it refused to switch to the euro. Even peddlers in the street and ladies looking after public toilets attempted to maintain the dignity of their national currency, zloty. Standing before the railway station in the downtown area, I felt as if I were in Moscow. The gray concrete buildings of Eastern European socialist countries looked as lifeless and depressing as army barracks. However, the concrete forest was dotted with brightly colored advertisements of capitalistic McDonald's and Coca Cola.

We were so unlucky that day that none of the people we asked on our way to the old town of Warsaw understood English. We had no other alternative but followed our gut and our map. When we finally got to the Market Square, we were greeted by a bronze plate with words in English, French, German, and Polish. The Warsaw Old Town was leveled to the ground by the German

Army at the turn of the season from summer into autumn in 1944, when the Polish resistance was defeated in the Warsaw Uprising. All buildings seen as they are today were reconstructions of the ones in the 1980s.

We stood in silence before the plate for a long time. In a week's time a magnificent castle first built in the Middle Ages was systematically blown up! People who live in peace and harmony would be absolutely terrified at the thought of the tragedy. Every building along the cobbled streets, including the Royal Castle and small pubs, bore on its exterior wall a picture of its state before the rebuilding. The bleak and desolate landscape reminds visitors of the horrifying autumn six decades before when no structure was left standing in the town.

It was burning hot in the square. To escape the heat, people began to move to the shade under the umbrella sunshades of the outdoor beer bars, with a group of kids left frolicking in the fountain's water at the center of the square. The beer with bubbles in it looked rather tempting, so when Joshua invited me for a cup of beer I accepted readily. I could think of nothing better than enjoying a cup of cold beer under the sunshade in the hot summer.

An old couple came toward us hand in hand. As the seats at our table were the only ones that they could choose, the husband turned to me. "Excuse me, Miss. May we take these seats?" "Oh, yes, of course," I rose and answered, "They aren't taken." I was surprised that in Warsaw someone spoke to me in English. It was obvious that Joshua was also interested in the old couple too and he offered to pay for their beer. The old man and his wife looked at each other before accepting it. Learning that I was from France, the wife looked rather enthusiastic with heightened color in her cheeks.

"Bonjour, vous être bienvenues en Pologne," she greeted me with unruffled calm. I was surprised at her perfect French.

As a journalist, I had the feeling that the couple meant to Joshua and me more than two people who spoke both English and French. I had noticed from the very beginning their unseasonal clothes: brown coarse uniforms, berets of the same color, white-and-red armbands on the left arm, and stickers of a logo on the chest featuring a combination of letters P and W. They looked as if they were shooting a movie about a battle.

The old man took a sip of his beer. "Have you ever heard of the Warsaw Uprising?" He asked. "Sixty-four years ago on August 1, 1944, the Home Army and Warsaw civilians launched an operation to liberate Warsaw from Nazi Germany. They fought for more than two months, but were defeated on October 2. More than two hundred thousand people died. Among the fifty thousand soldiers killed and missing were over four thousand women."

Evina's father was a Polish diplomat based in France before the Second World War. Living in Paris in their childhood, Evina and her two sisters spoke French as naturally as native Frenchmen. Their father was later removed from his position due to his anti-war opinions expressed before the public when the war broke out. When the family returned to Warsaw, the black flag of the Nazi Empire was everywhere, driving locals mad. In the spring of 1944, her father was no longer depressed. He was excited, to be exact. He tuned to the Soviet radio to learn about the daily advance of the Red Army towards the eastern suburb of the city.

He even secretly taught her daughters the song prepared for the rebellion. He told them that Nazi Germany would be defeated and that Poland had to fight to liberate Warsaw from the Nazis as soon as possible, instead of sitting at home waiting for the Soviet army to help.

Her father and mother busied themselves in their yard in the days at the end of July by filling bottles with petrol to make napalm and cutting white cotton curtains into strips to be used to bandage wounds. They even packed a bag of kitchen knives and forks as weapons. On the first night of August, the parents left home with their eldest daughters, and Evina was told to meet the Red Army in a place on the bank of the Vistula River.

The Vistula runs through Warsaw from the northwest of the city to the southeast. In summer the beaches were full of people, and Evina and her sisters learned their swimming skills in the river. Evina was rather excited because her father told her that she would be a national heroine if she could manage to bring a letter to the spearhead of the Soviet army. She thought that her father entrusted her with the vital task probably because she spoke better Russian than her sisters. She crossed the river by way of the Gdańsk Bridge at night and resourcefully found the Russian army. However, she couldn't figure out why the spearhead troop refused to ford the river.

The rebellion was met by intense attack from the Germans, and Adolf Hitler claimed that his troops would wipe Warsaw from the world map. The main formation of Nazi Germany that arrived at Warsaw from the West Line turned the city into a sea of fire. The Gdańsk Bridge was destroyed and Evina could not get across the river to go back home.

"Go for my family," she pleaded again and again with the Soviet woman soldier. "They could be killed by Germans." However, no one paid attention to her. In a global war which involved millions of people, the voice of a little girl was nothing.

Two months later, the uprising was heavily defeated, with more than two hundred thousand Polish bodies lying on the ground of their own land. Evina never saw her family again. Their names were now on the memorial wall established in honor of those who died in the rebellion.

It was getting late in the afternoon, and the wind in the square became cooler. More seniors of Evina's age came, with the same armband around the left arms and the same sticker on their chest. The music for the uprising was played and the veterans lined up in shaky steps in the middle of the square. They started to sing in their plaintive, melancholy voice, to honor their lost family members and battle companions in the war.

Joshua and I couldn't understand the lyrics, but tears streamed down our cheeks. The song was sung with heart and soul by people who survived bloody battles.

A mock camouflage tank came, with young men and women playing soldiers who were injured on the head or in the arm. They showed how fighters in the war sixty-four years ago chose death before disgrace when they ran out of ammunition and provisions.

"Miss, do you know the history of the Warsaw Uprising?" A young woman came to me with a sticker that the old couple had in her palm. "Would you like to have a sticker to honor our heroes who died in the war?"

"Yes, of course. I'm Chinese and I don't know much of your city, but I believe any blood for justice in human history will never be shed in vain." I put the sticker on my chest and so did Joshua. He even had an armband on his left arm. We were invited to board the tank, and I imagined that I was one of the two hundred thousand soldiers.

Evina and her husband came over to have a photo taken together with us. "Miss, you're a journalist," her husband told me. "Would you please tell China and the world that the Warsaw people are people with integrity? We do whatever is needed for our country and our nation."

"My grandfather fought against Fascists, too. He bears on his leg a scar from a Japanese bullet," I said. After saying goodbye to the old couple, we went in the tank to the memorial wall beside Andre Avenue. A candlelit vigil would be held in honor of the war victims. The uprising memorial wall is made of dark green glass into which millions of names are carved. While I ran my hands over the names on the wall, it seemed as if I could see before my eyes those men, women, and children.

"Yao Yao, don't you think this is fate that it is the anniversary of the Warsaw Uprising before we go to Auschwitz?" Joshua asked me. "This has to be preparing us for even more tragedy." I nodded in agreement.

# 4

There was a long line at the information desk in the central railway station of Warsaw, the only place where foreigners could go for information in English. When I asked the middle-age man about the train schedules for Kraków, he smiled and printed a list of timetable for all the trains to the city. Express trains to Kraków were operated on a two-hour basis.

Excited, we immediately decided to buy tickets for the 2:00 p.m. train. However, no information was available about our train when it was well past one o'clock. I went to information again, but the middle-age man was replaced by a rather plump lady who did not understand English. She explained loudly in Polish, with various hand gestures when two Asian faces appeared before me. The younger one told me tentatively that he and his father were from Japan and they were on their way to Kyiv, the capital of Ukraine. He told me that no message for their 1:30 p.m. train was displayed yet, so I could take it easy. I then understood that the timetables at the station were only for reference as the trains seldom came on time.

When we returned to the waiting room, the Japanese men were reading stories. Obviously, that was not their first time taking a train in Warsaw. As it could be expected, a message for our train appeared on the display screen at half past two, saying the train would be on platform three. Joshua jumped for my luggage, while hurrying me up. We said goodbye to the Japanese father and son and ran to the platform, only to find it was encumbered by passengers coming in from all directions while the train was still yet to come. We waited for about twenty minutes before the train pulled in with a loud noise. A man in uniform came out and shouted "Kraków, Kraków," with his arms waving up and down as if he were chasing a flock of ducks. When the train came to a complete halt, the passengers swarmed into the train and the platform soon resumed its quietness.

It was an express train, but travelers were not required to sit according to the numbers on the seats. Those who came in late stood on the corridor without a murmur, with their hands on the window to appreciate the scenery outside. This reminded me of the Spring Festival traffic in China. Joshua and I were early enough to find two seats opposite to each other. Drying the sweat on my face, I said to Joshua, "Poland is an EU member, but the railway system here is so different from those in France." He shrugged his shoulders as if to say that we should not complain about the system in Warsaw, which suffered so much in the past that any inconvenience we suffered here deserved our forgiveness.

Polish express trains were not divided into soft and hard seats, and the cars were partitioned into separated compartments, in each of which were six seats. Outside the sliding doors was a corridor down one side. When we entered the car, a gray hair lady in a smart dress edged with youthful lace was waving a folding silk fan before her face. She did not bother to raise her eyes as we entered, as if we were not welcome in her compartment. Seeing the bottom of Joshua's T-shirt swelled out when he tried to place our luggage on the overhead rack, she immediately covered her nose with her fan, wrinkling her brows as if she was offended by his body odor. Joshua apologized again and again, but she refused to turn her head at him.

A young couple appeared in the corridor with two big carrying cases. Dripping with perspiration, they looked around for seats. We could hear they were whispering to each other in French. As there were two vacant seats in our compartment and there was space on the rack for more luggage, Joshua looked out to greet the couple, ignoring the dirty look on the lady's face. The young wife was so excited that she blew Joshua a kiss before coming in with her husband. I noticed the old lady had closed her eyes, while her nose was still buried in her fan. She must have grown up in a wealthy family, I thought. I didn't tell Joshua what I had in mind, because Poles of noble birth understood French.

To express their appreciation, the wife tore open a bag of preserves and offered them to us.

The lady shook her head with her eyes slightly open, wearing a sneering expression on her face. Indiscreetly, the husband began to enjoy his potato chips. In no time, an acrid smell of sweat, sweetness, and onion filled the air in the crowded compartment. The smells made the place even more claustrophobic in a train without air conditioning or even an electric fan in the height of summer, and I somewhat felt sorry for the old lady.

The French speaking wife was Polish and her Belgian husband accompanied her to visit her parents in Kraków. After they learned that we were going on to Auschwitz, the young wife started to draw a map for us on a piece of paper. Upon hearing the name of "Auschwitz," the old lady suddenly opened her eyes, while she sat in complete silence.

It was quite baffling that the nonstop train stopped when we were about 100 kilometers away from Kraków. The train conductors were nowhere to be found. Joshua and the young couple found it a great opportunity to enjoy a smoke outside the train. While I offered to stay to look after the luggage, I found it a chance to start a conversation with the lady.

A group of retired soldiers with shaved heads on their way back home got off the train and let off steam by singing and shouting. "Life in barracks is depressing, and people who are set free are crazy with excitement," the lady suddenly said to herself.

I was surprised that she was speaking in French, and I was sure she meant to speak to me. I had been right that most senior Poles from wealthy families understood French.

To initiate a conversation, I started to compliment her on her dress by saying it accentuated her elegance and gracefulness. I immediately regretted my foolhardy move because I found myself talking to someone who was remarkably reserved as if she were my next door neighbor. But it seemed she was waiting for my fulsome compliments. She hitched up the hem of her dress. "I did it all by myself," she said with pride. "I started to make dresses with lace when I was a girl. I once made a lace wedding dress for a bride." While she let go of her dress, she asked me: "Miss, are you really going to Auschwitz? Do Chinese people know about the death camp in Poland?"

"Yes, of course, Madame. What happened

there should be remembered by all human beings. Auschwitz should never be forgotten." I chose my words with great care.

"For Poles, Auschwitz is a permanent scab," she said as she let out a long sigh. "It bleeds whenever you touch it."

Elsa was born in a small town in the southern suburb of Kraków. Her mother, an intelligent woman who had a pair of willing hands, managed a successful tailor shop. Sometimes Elsa worked as a helper for her mother when they stayed at the house of a wealthy family to finish an order. When the mother busied herself with a wedding gown one year at the turn of summer into autumn, Elsa helped with the border patterns. When she finished her work, she added on her own creation of two strips of lace of different widths along the neckline. The bride found she looked gorgeous when she tried in on and invited Elsa to her wedding.

It was a typical wedding ceremony in southern Poland. Before darkness came the bride danced with each of the guests who were older than she was. Everyone at the occasion spoke highly of the bride's dress, saying it was the fanciest wedding gown ever in the town, which filled Elsa with great pride.

The ceremony was reaching its high point when a truck with German SS soldiers halted before the gate. The officer announced in German that they were told that the bride was half-Jewish and therefore should go with them to a concentration camp. Her father-in-law went over attempting to explain, but was pushed away by a soldier with his gun butt. A soldier took the bride by her lace neckline, dragged her along and loaded her onto the truck, as if a tiger was carrying its prey home. A joyous celebratory occasion was turned into a tragedy, and the bridegroom ran after the departing truck in desperation but was stopped by the guests, who feared that he may be shot by the SS soldiers in whom humanity had been long lost.

Elsa learned later from her mother and her neighbors that the young woman was shipped to Auschwitz and gassed with her wedding gown on. With the black smoke hung over the town, Auschwitz was a nightmare in the years between 1940 and 1945.

Finally the train was about to move on, and the

passengers on the ground rushed in. The steely look resumed on Elsa's face. When the train stopped at the Kraków station, she said to me: "Thank you, Miss China, for your visit to Auschwitz. It's a long way, isn't it?"

"Good for you, Yao Yao," Joshua said with surprise when the lady left the car. "You're a qualified journalist! She said goodbye to you."

"Do you know what it cost you to smoke outside the train? You missed a story about the Auschwitz camp. Anyway, you can hear it for a cup of cool beer when we are in Kraków."

I kept him guessing what had happened when he was away.

## 5

Joshua and I lived in the Warszawa Grand Hotel opposite the railway station at Kraków. With guest rooms as high as four to five meters, the hotel looked like a palace. The young woman at the reception spoke some Chinese and she told me she would visit China next year. Joshua and I paid the same money, but my room was twice as large as his.

In the evening we went to buy our tickets for an early train to Auschwitz. The booking office clerk told us in English that, unlike the trains in Warsaw, their trains followed the schedule to the letter, which delighted us.

Kraków was once the Polish capital and it escaped from the gunfire of the Second World War. The regal buildings in the old town remained what they had been in the eighteenth century and nearly half of them had on their walls the logo of the heritage protection department. Joshua honored his promise by inviting me for a cold beer in an outside restaurant encircled by rose bushes. And I honored mine by telling him the story that Elsa had told. Joshua sat in gloomy silence after I finished. I knew it was because we were approaching our destination.

Since the Auschwitz Museum opened, the railway line from Kraków to the small town became a most busy line in the country. We boarded the earliest train in the morning. The seats in the empty coach were scruffy, and the window glasses had numerous cracks in them, looking as if they would collapse anytime when the train was clanking and rattling over the rails.

"This is an old train, but it must be in better condition than the cattle trains used to ship Jews to the camp, isn't it?" Joshua said with a laugh. "We would have no idea about how they suffered on their way if we sit more comfortably in a cushioned berth sleeping car."

I saw what he meant. Travelers visit the concentration camp to update the meaning of the word "humanity" in their dictionaries, in the same way they attend a lecture about the value of life. The trip can be anything but a treat of leisurely traveling.

I asked whether the steel rails were used to ship Jewish inmates, and Joshua answered with a "probably." During the period between 1940 and 1945, numerous rails in Europe were connected with Poland, with Auschwitz as their terminus.

It took our old train three hours to cover the sixty kilometers from Kraków to Auschwitz. The town was small and quiet, and the station was about the size of three retail stores, smaller than a common station in a remote village in China. When I was approaching the station shop, the salesgirl handed over a map of the town, as if she knew what I had in mind. She must know that it was the Nazi death camp that attracted international tourists to her town.

With the map in my hand, it was easy for us to find the bus stop. We had barely gotten on the bus when we were asked "Auschwitz?" by the driver. He spoke in Polish, but all foreigners knew what he referred to. A woman asked us "Auschwitz?" and then pointed to a path when we were about to ask her which road we should take. All visitors in town shared one purpose, the Auschwitz Museum.

Different from many museums in the world, the Auschwitz Museum were free for visitors. No tickets are required for people who come to honor humanity by remembering the four million victims.

Joshua and I both had a bunch of yellow roses in our backpacks in honor of the dead. Joshua wrote down on the register at the entrance the name of the sister of his great grandmother. In 1945 when the Soviet Red Army moved into the camp, they discovered four hundred thousand copies of files of Jewish inmates. These documents have been computerized, making it easier for family members or descendants of the prisoners to find their information. The friendly receptionist suggested that Joshua come back for the result when he finished his tour in the museum.

I stood before the front gate of the concentration camp, an iron gate with an arch with the infamous camp slogan that crowned the entrance: Arbeit Macht Frei. I had seen the gate many times in movies and pictures. The slogan aroused the desire to make it alive in the mind of all Jewish inmates when they were shipped to the camp along the route of the Death March. The lie was that they would have the opportunity to come out of the camp when they worked hard enough to meet the Nazi standards. We are Jewish people and we are not afraid of hard work, they must have thought.

It was a sunny day in a hot summer, but I felt a cold shiver down my spine because I was with a heavy heart. This was Auschwitz I, where the three-story barracks were the museum's exhibition rooms. I had to take a deep breath and give myself a mental shake before I went into a barrack unit, so that I could stay long enough to go over the exhibits in the room. On a black marble counter was a name list of more four hundred thousand Jewish inmates at the camp. It was a typewritten list and stood more than thirty centimeters. It was hard for me to imagine that the Nazis could keep a neat list of the prisoners before they murdered them. The victims included in the list were lucky in the sense that their family members or relatives are able to know about the last days of their lives, but the lives extinguished in the crematoriums left no clues for their families. "Yao Yao, do you think we can find Yura on the list?" Joshua asked me.

"Yes, I think so. You would not come such a long way in vain." I took a firm grip of his hand.

In a huge glass case in the barracks room was a display of thousands of shoes taken from the victims. Among them were men's boots, girl's high heeled leather sandals, and toddler's shoes with soft soles. Every pair of the shoes represents a life before he or she was murdered. Closing my eyes, I could just picture their appearances in my mind. A pair of rosy red leather kitten heels with red leather bowknots near the tips stood out among them.

They must be popular even with the girls of today, I thought.

Joshua fixed his eyes on the kitten heels too. He turned to me with a curious look on his face. We had the same question in mind: "Were they Yura's?" They must match the young and elegant Yura I saw in the photo. I tried to convince myself that I had made a valid guess and, at the same time, it was too cruel for me to expect another girl in her early youth who had suffered the same fate.

As is shown in books and documentaries, Jewish inmates were stripped of all personal possessions, including jewelry, gold teeth, even hair, before they were murdered. To own a carpet made of human hair was considered an indicator of a life of luxury in Germany during the Second World War. I was totally shocked by this startling fact on the explanation board: while the hair of an average of fifty adults weighs about one kilo, a total of one thousand nine-hundred fifty kilos of the hair was displayed in the case. My tears brimmed over and rolled slowly down my cheeks to the ground, like drops of blood from my broken heart.

Joshua jabbed me with his elbow, gesturing

towards the right side of the case. Standing out in the shade of dark gray of the hair due to passage of time was a thick four-strand ribbon braid, lying there in silence like a work of art. It must had have kept for years before it was shorn from the head of a girl, who tried to keep up with fashion. For more than six decades the braid had been lying there with its faded blue silk bowknot at the end, hopelessly waiting for its owner, who had cherished it.

Standing beside me was a middle age couple. Facing the display case, the wife was quietly sobbing in pain, and the husband touched her hair subconsciously before his hand slid down and rested lightly on her shoulder. "All has long passed. The tragedy won't be repeated."

I dried my tears and followed the crowd from one display to another: thousands and thousands of pairs of glasses, suitcases with owners' names on them, one-piece jumpsuits for babies. Some of the victims had unfinished novels with them, and some were with their saxophones. They believed in what the gate slogan said: "Work sets you free." Freedom was the luxury of luxuries for inmates in the camp.

I felt numb all over. My tears had never

stopped sliding down my cheeks, but I refused to wipe them. I shivered even in the summer heat of thirty-five degree Celsius outside the exhibition rooms. So did Joshua, who had remained silence for nearly an hour, wrestling with the emotional pain he had never felt before.

The receptionist stopped us when we were coming out of the Auschwitz I museum. "Mr. Joshua, would you please go to the Birkenau museum as quickly as possible? Several survivors are arriving and you might want to ask them some questions."

Joshua and I were delighted at the news. We thanked her and rushed to the free transfer bus. The two museums were three kilometers apart and the bus operated on an hourly basis. When we approached the bus, it was about to leave and the driver stuck his hand out of the window waving to us. The bus was packed like sardines, and the passengers bunched together to make space for each other.

Auschwitz II used to be the main camp, with a size several tenfold that of Auschwitz I. Standing on the primary guard tower to the entrance of the camp, I saw numerous rows of barracks for Jewish inmates on the boundless plain and the barbed wire fences stretching out as far as the eye could see. The infamous route of the Death March along the main road in the camp, which transported millions of Jews to the living hell, was left intact after the liberation of Auschwitz on January 27, 1945. The rails were covered with rust, and wildflowers scattered in the space between wooden ties. At the end of the rails were two tracts leading to the left and right sides. When the cattle trains stopped and the prisoners were forced to exit, they were selected by German doctors. Those who were physically fit went to the right to the slave camp, but the sick, the weak, the old, and most women and children proceeded down the left track to the gas chambers, which were connected with the crematoriums. The photos taken by Germans when the camp was in operation were placed beside the tracks, showing the same place where I was.

A gray-haired old man was approaching us, followed by a group of soldiers with martial bearings. Joshua told me the old man was speaking Hebrew. He went over to greet the old man and asked if we could join them. In no time we were among the group members, listening to the old man's stories. The soldiers kindly suggested the two of us sit beside the old man. Of course, they didn't know that I didn't understand Hebrew.

## 6

The Larbi family managed a silver shop in the old town of Kraków. The shop was started more than one hundred years ago, when silver jewelry were popular among women in southern Poland during the years between the mid and the late nineteenth century. At that time, silver served as a must for rings, earrings, necklaces, and ornaments in the waists, collars, and sleeve openings.

When Mr. Larbi became the owner of the family business, the shop was three times as large in size, with the shop facing the street and the backyard as the workshop. In addition to its traditional jewelry trade, production and sales of silver kitchenware dominated the business. When the whole of Poland was occupied by German

Nazis at the end of 1940, the freedom of Jewish people became increasingly limited. The glass in several windows of the shop were broken and "Go away Jewish pigs" and other insulting words were dabbed on the outside wall, as a well-known local brand, the business continued.

Mr. Larbi paused and stared at me, and then he continued with difficulty in his English. "You know what? I had in my shop two craftsmen from China. They were father and son, which I called 'Old Zhang' and 'Little Zhang.' Old Zhang went to France as a laborer after the First World War to build railways. Little Zhang was born there in France. When the Second World War broke out, the father and son worked even harder to earn the money they needed to return to China. But how could they when the transportation to Asia was almost broken down? When they were later stranded penniless in Kraków, I took them in. Little Zhang didn't read much, but he was skillful with his hands. In a short time he learned how to make silver items, and from time to time he surprised me with new styles of decorations."

Hardly had Mr. Larbi finished when a young

military officer cut in. "Chinese and Jews share one thing: they are more intelligent than others." His remarks were met with a ripple of delighted laughter, before we shared the old man's traumatic story of what happened later to him and his friends.

It was a day at the turn from autumn to winter, when a German officer came to his shop with a sizable check. He ordered twelve sets of silver kitchen utensils, which needed to be delivered in three days. The craftsmen worked day and night and finished the order before the deadline. Mr. Larbi, along with Old Zhang and Little Zhang, delivered the kitchen items in three big bags to an apartment in the downtown area. When they entered the building, they were immediately put onto a truck, which transferred them to a cattle destined to Auschwitz. Mr. Larbi was trapped by Germans probably because of the fame of his business. The shop owner and his Chinese workers simply disappeared in the morning, but no one knew the place to which they were sent.

The three of them were order to get off the train at the end of the route of the Death March.

A German doctor with a pair of glasses over a crooked nose checked their eyelids with his hand and their teeth ridges with a small hammer before he tipped his head to one side, indicating they belonged to the work camp. If the head had moved to the other side, they would have been sent to the gas chambers.

I was sitting on the rails of the Death March when the old man told his stories. About twenty meters from us was a circular ditch about three meters deep and five meters wide. Over the ditch there used to be a barbed wire fence about four meters high, which was electrified in those years when it was getting dark. Birds would be burned when they were not careful as they crossed the fence. The ditch and the wire netting served as a double insurance measure to prevent prisoners from escaping from the camp.

Mr. Larbi and his two Chinese craftsmen as a group were assigned the work to dig and move earth, with Mr. Larbi and Old Zhang digging the earth and Little Zhang moving it. On the ground above their trench were German soldiers followed by their fierce attack dogs, who usually hanged their red tongues out. The dogs were familiar with the prisoners, so they would bark to signal the soldiers for anyone who was away from his work site.

While working, Old Zhang told Mr. Larbi: "It is quite baffling that the three of us were sent here for slave labor. If we don't escape from here, we will be sent to the gas chambers."

Larbi replied with a sigh: "I'm Jewish, and it seems I will never escape from German hands. I compromised you and your son. You are Chinese and you don't belong here."

One day when the prisoners gathered for roll call before dinner, Larbi risked his life to intercede before a German guard for the father and the son, who, he thought, should be set free. The guard slapped him on the face and cried: "Chinese are fighting against Japan, who is our Axis partner. China is our enemy. These two belong to jail or they should be killed."

Being desperate, they decided to risk their lives to escape. While working, they observed for opportunities. On the west of the camp was a rectangle pond with a storage capacity of a couple of scores of cubic meters. There was a gap of about three meters wide in the wire along the pond. But every movement could be observed by the guard when the searchlight on the watchtower was turned on at night. The germ of an escape plan formed. The three would hide themselves in the water near the edge of the bank when they stopped work at sunset, so that they could camouflage in the bushes while keeping their heads above water for air.

It was a moonless night and a strong wind was blowing when they went ahead with their plan, a rare chance to escape. Unfortunately, an inmate in their barracks reported to the guard when he found three of his fellow inmates missing, in the hope that his deed would help to set him free. The guards immediately searched along the wire fence, with the help of all their dogs.

Old Zhang told Larbi: "I'm too old to run fast. You're younger and you are able to run away with my son."

But soon he and his son were discovered by the sharp nose of a dog, which pulled them out of water with its mouth. They were shot dead on the spot. Frightened, Larbi swam underwater until he reached a dark outer corner, where he bobbed up and breathed hard.

Mr. Larbi rose from the rails and a large group of people followed him to the pond. It was dry and fresh grass grew in the mud at the bottom. Walking around the pond, the old man told us: "This is the place where I escaped. The Chinese father and his son didn't give me away and they were killed. The Jewish informer was killed, too. You know they had to kill three prisoners. Many years later I learned about what happened after I ran away."

When he finished, Larbi took out a red bag from his pocket. In it was an egg-sized white porcelain paperweight with blue flowers, patterns resembling the blue and white porcelain ware popular in China. It was a gift from Old Zhang, and for more than six decades Mr. Larbi had carried it with him, in honor of the Chinese father and his son, who helped with his narrow escape.

After his successful escape, Larbi soon joined the Polish Underground Army. He finally settled down in the Soviet Ukraine. When the Second World War ended, he engaged in trade and later became one of the top ten billionaires in the country. He opened a township porcelain factory in Zhejiang Province in the 1990s, as he vaguely remembered that Old Zhang was from a place called Zhejiang. The father and his son died in a foreign land, but Larbi hoped that their nostalgic dreams had come true.

When we were about to leave, I felt a blast of cool air and I saw the old man's gray hair streaming in the wind. He shook my hand and said: "Miss Journalist, it has been assuring to meet a Chinese person again at Auschwitz more than sixty years later. Our Jewish people would never forget the help from the Chinese people during the Second World War. The two nations share the cultural tradition of treating kindness with kindness."

A tear rolled down my cheek. I could picture groups of people like Larbi and Old Zhang and his son, who were driven to desperation and death in the camp. Suddenly I realized that it was wrong for me to see myself as a visitor at Auschwitz. All the people who live in peace today, including Joshua and I, shared the same life community on the planet with the victims of the massacre, and our lives were equally valuable.

# 7

Joshua and I decided to spend a few more days in the town. While he was waiting for clues about Yura from the museum, I hoped to contact more survivors from the massacre.

We stayed in a three-story family hotel, with the family of the owner living in the first floor. Summer was the tourist season at Auschwitz, and family hotels were always full because they were cheaper. A lady in her seventies and his son checked in a few minutes later than we did, and they had to share my neighboring room. She used the bed and her son, who was nearly fifty, had to sleep on the floor. As the rooms were not well soundproofed, I could hear they were speaking in French, which aroused my curiosity as to why they came to visit the town. After all, I could communicate with them in French.

The hotel provided a substantial breakfast for guests, with quite a few choices for coffee and cheese. Slices of bread were coming out from a toaster. When I was enjoying my toast with butter and cheese, the old lady living next door entered

the dining room, all by herself. It was only at that
time that I realized she was only about 1.4 meters
tall. She wanted to take a piece of toast, but she
found it difficult for her to reach the plate beside
the machine. I immediately went over and asked in
French: "Madame, let me help. How many pieces
do you want?"

"Oh, yes. It's very nice of you. You speak
French? Were you born in France?"

"No. I'm a Chinese journalist, and I work in
France." I helped her with a couple of toast and a
cup of cereal with milk. When we sat down at a
table, Joshua came over with his plate. I told him
about the lady and her son.

The lady was frank and talkative, and in a few
minutes I learned about her purpose to visit the
town. She was a survivor of the genocide; her name
was Opeia; she was from Geneva, Switzerland. To
visit the death camp, where she spent several years
of her childhood, had been the strongest will in her
remaining years.

Puzzled at her motives for the trip, I asked:
"You were treated inhumanly at the concentration
camp, which have left deep scars. Why do you wish

to come back more than half a century later?"

Putting her spoon down, she patted on my knee: "Miss, I'm not afraid of coming back to Auschwitz. God blessed us and my brothers and sisters made it alive from this living hell. There is no reason for me to be afraid. I came back for all my brothers and sisters."

When she spoke to us, her son buried his head in his milk glass. I didn't know how many times in his life he has heard his mother telling her stories in the death camp, but his silence implied his tacit consent to her agreement to recall the fateful days in her life before two strangers, which must be extremely painful for her.

Opeia was the youngest of the seven children in her family. All the other six suffered from achondroplasia, a common cause of dwarfism. Her father, a dentist in Switzerland, hoped his youngest daughter would grow taller than the others, and Opeia had been cosseted in the family ever since she was born. In the summer of 1944 when anti-Semitism in Germany reached its peak, Opeia and her family fell into the evil hands of the Nazis and were transported to the death camp at

Auschwitz, despite the fact that Switzerland was a neutral country and Geneva was an international city.

Immediately after their arrival and the selection, Opeia's parents, along with many other Jewish inmates, perished in gas chambers and crematoriums. Because they were normal adults, they were not related by the Nazis at the camp to the seven dwarves, who were taken by the German physician Josef Mengele to his clinic at a corner of the camp. "No one will attempt to murder you if you're with me, doing what I ask you to do," he told them. Except for Opeia, all her brothers and sisters had passed their puberty, and they were able to understand what the physician meant. In a living hell where crematoriums belched out black smoke and other inmates were forced to do slave labor, driven by fear of death the seven dwarfs had no other alternative but obey Doctor Mengele's orders, allowing him to perform any experiment on their bodies.

He sheared their hair and later their eyelashes for his experiments. They suffered terribly from the resulted orbital cellulitis and abscess, and they had a burning pain even when they blinked their eyes. Doctor Mengele even pulled their teeth out without anesthesia. When her newly grown teeth were removed, Opeia bled heavily from the wounds, but instead of screaming her head off, she chose to swallow the blood.

The physician had never explained why those experiments were done on them. One day the eldest brother plucked up enough courage and asked: "Doctor Mengele, when will you set us free?"

The doctor answered with a sneering smile: "You've been more than fortunate not having been sent to a crematorium. You know it's me who helped you. How ridiculous that you have the idea of going back home! Jews shouldn't have homes, you know."

It was only when doctor Mengele was away for his dinner or snap that the seven of them had a chance to watch what was happening outside the window with steel bars. The camp had long been free of children and occasionally they could see a couple of shadowy figures moving before the barracks in the distance. No one else in the camp knew seven dwarfs were imprisoned in the experiment lab, and the doctor warned them constantly that to step out of the building was to lose his protection, which meant to court death.

The winter came early in southern Poland in 1944, and in early December the ground was already covered with a thick layer of snow. For days doctor Mengele wore an uneasy expression on his face and left the brothers and sisters alone, busying himself sorting his experiment results and packing them into several big carrying cases, which were once possessions of Jewish inmates.

Opeia still remembered what the doctor told them, the seven subjects for his medical experiments, before he fled to Berlin with his documents on a cold night: "You suffered in my experimental surgeries, but you should remember me as your savior. Without my idea to do experiments on you for medical research, freaks of nature like you would have been dead years ago."

The Soviet Red Army moved into the death camp on January 27, 1945. Several soldiers from a tank forced into Doctor Mengele's laboratory, and they were flabbergasted at what they saw: the seven dying "children." They were puzzled because it had been reported that no children were left in the camp.

The oldest of the seven could spoke some Russian and he explained what happened to them in the camp. They were soon sent to the Soviet Union to recuperate, before they returned to Switzerland in the late 1950s. Now Opeia was the only of the siblings who were still alive.

With her hand covered with liver spots, Opeia wiped her tears away. "My six siblings were all shorter than I am. They remained single till the end of their days and they died before they reached forty. I've been the luckiest among my siblings. I've been married with a family. My son is tall and strong, you see. He now has children of his own." Her quiet son then put his arm around her neck and patted her gently as if she were a baby.

Joshua stood up and went over to Opeia. "Madame, I'm a member of Operation: Last Chance. We are trying to track down Nazi criminals. Do you want to know more about Doctor Mengele?"

Hearing the name of Josef Mengele, the old lady gave a shiver of fear, staring at Joshua with her mouth wide open.

When Josef Mengele went back to Berlin, he left the Nazi army and started a clinic. With growing calls to capture war criminals that tortured or murdered Jews, fearing being captured, Mengele escaped and finally settled in Argentina with his family in an attempt to evade justice. He stayed incognito in Buenos Aires, making a living by running a toy shop in a quiet neighborhood. No one in the community had ever related the genial owner of the shop to the genocide at Auschwitz. Instead, the children loved him, because he gave them cheap small toys for nothing.

One day in the 1990s, Josef Mengele received a letter from Operation: Last Chance, with photographs of him at work at Auschwitz. He was told his article about degeneration of Jewish people had been found in some universities and medical institutions in Berlin, damning evidence of his medical experiments on Jewish inmates to search for physiological support for Nazi mass murder of Jews. The letter urged Mengele to surrender to the police, warning him of an accusation against him at the International Court of Justice.

The following day Mengele was found drowned in his swimming pool, and no one was sure whether he lost his footing or committed suicide.

Opeia told us that the purpose of her visit to Auschwitz was two-fold: to help her son with a better understanding of her traumatic memories of what she suffered at the camp and, more importantly, to meet an old friend, Kokov, the Red Army soldier who saved the lives of the seven dwarfs sixty-three years before.

Joshua and I felt an irresistible impulse to kiss the old lady, as we were so lucky to encounter at the hotel the survivor of the death camp and her son.

# 8

At noon on the third day, the eighty-one years old Kokov arrived for his meeting. The veteran was tall and grey-haired. He was slow to move, but his steps were rather firm, reminding me of the soldier he was when he was young. He opened his arms to greet Opeia. "How are you, little girl? Who has expected we could meet more than sixty years later at Auschwitz?"

Opeia was as tall as Kokov's chest, and her tears wetted the bottom of his shirt. He repeated what he did when he entered the death camp by patting on her head and said: "The Soviet Red Army troops are here for you."

It was the night of January 26, 1945. The eighteen year old Kokov, a soldier of the spearhead of the Red Army Division 322, along with five of his partners, was ordered to attack a place marked "Auschwitz" on their map. When he got out of his tank, he saw a place with barbed wire fences and a German slogan that spanned the entrance, which said Arbeit Macht Frei. Having no idea about the place, they pushed the door open with great care, while tightening their fingers on the triggers of their automatics, which held close to their chests. It was eerily quiet, and a suffocating acrid stink of burnt flesh permeated the air. One of them guessed correctly. "Is this the German camp for Jews? I remember the leaflet mentioned the name of 'Auschwitz.'"

Before them stood rows of wooden barracks on the snow covered ground, with a chimney on the roof of each unit. The barracks had no windows and no smoke was coming out the chimneys. Kokov had no idea what they were used for. It must be freezing in them if no fire was kept inside, he thought. They forced a door open. It was empty, but with blood and cabbage on the floor, looking as if it was a deserted slaughter house.

Kokov saw what he would never forget in his whole life, when he followed a partner's voice to a row of barracks far back. A group of inmates in worn-out stripped outfit waved their hands to the soldiers. Their faces were reduced to a skull, with protruding eyes. They looked like human-looking animals, Kokov thought. Some of them had rags from sack bags over them, and others wore dirty hats. They waved their hands with great effort and shouted in coarse voices in foreign languages. When Kokov and his partners got closer, they could see clearly the vessels under the skin in their hands which stretched out. It seemed that the bones and joints in their arms were not covered by skin but placed in a plastic bag.

A crippled inmate came over to Kokov, or crawl over to him, to be exact. He touched Kokov's leg and tried to shout: "Spaseebo, tovarish (Thank you, comrade)." Kokov was so surprised at hearing the prisoner speaking his own language that he helped him up and fed him with his water bottle. In broken sentences, the inmate told Kokov and his partners what had happened to the survivors.

The place they were in was called Auschwitz II-Birkenau, the largest camp at Auschwitz. The Germans had been gone, but before their retreat they shot into the barracks with machine guns and blew up the two largest gas chambers. They were also ordered to set all the camps on fire in an attempt to hide their crimes, but thanks to the direction of the wind and the snow at night, these inmates survived the massacre.

More Soviet troops came and the survivors were moved to houses with fire. The soldiers prepared dozens of pots of soup and several baskets of bread for them. The Russian inmate had been a Red Army soldier but he was captured in battle. With his help, Russian soldiers were able to ride their jeep to research every nook and cranny of the camp.

On an open ground in the west of the camp

were bundles of firewood with corpses between them, an unfinished task to hide their crimes. There were also trolleys with dead bodies along the rails leading to the crematoriums, where the pipes were still warm. In several warehouses they searched were tons of human hair, glass lenses, shoes, and gold teeth yanked out from the mouths of the inmates who had been murdered.

It was at this time when Kokov encountered Opeia and her sisters and brothers, who cowered in a corner, looking thoroughly frightened. Kokov handed over several pieces of bread, and they immediately started to wolf them down. The eldest brother ate a little and put the rest secretly under his straw mattress, so that the seven of them had something to eat in the next few days. He didn't know Auschwitz had been liberated from Nazi Germany. Kokov told them by way of his fellow countryman that after the liberation they didn't have to go hungry and all prisoners would leave the camp alive.

Kokov was later ordered to take care of the camp and the survivors. Doctors and nurses were sent to do physical examinations or treat the survivors. It was curious that none of them would take a bath. They would shiver involuntarily with fear and desperation in their eyes when soap and towel was offered. The Russian survivor explained the reason behind it to Kokov: Nazis built gas chambers and crematoriums to improve their murder process of Jews. The gas chambers were decorated with white ceramic tiles and equipped with tower facilities. But when Jewish inmates turned on the shower, poison gas was turned on. To fool the prisoners to be murdered, Jewish inmates were sent to hand out soap and towels among their fellow prisoners, who would accept them without much hesitation.

Several years later, Kokov was invited by the International Court of Justice to attend the trials at Nuremberg and he learned that up to 1.1 million inmates were murdered from 1940 to 1945, the majority of them killed in gas chambers and crematoriums.

As I thought it would be too cruel to have two seniors over seventy recall their hellish nightmares at Auschwitz, I suggested a walk outside. "Let's walk from here to the remains of Auschwitz II-Birkenau," said Kokov. It was decided soon after the truth of the death camp was publicized by the Red Army that the hell on earth be kept to warn future generations against similar crimes.

The town of Auschwitz looked gorgeous in the sunny day, with trees along almost every road. The locals loved flowers and flowerpots were hung outside windows or gates, looking as if the owners grew them to please passersby. Pointing to a gravel path, Kokov told us: "It is along this path I rode my tank towards the gate of the camp. The path is just what it was more than sixty years ago. For numerous times it appeared in my dream."

We followed Mr. Kokov in the hot afternoon to the remains of the crematoriums at a corner of the camp, which were destroyed by Germans before they fled. With no single brick removed in the past years, the site was heart shattering for each and every visitor. Beside the remains, there stood a memorial made of large pieces of rock, with the inscription of "NEVER FORGET, NEVER AGAIN."

Joshua and I insisted on taking the two survivors to lunch in a small restaurant and they agreed. Joshua, Opeia's son, Kokov's daughter, and I proposed a toast to Opeia and Kokov, who suffered in the world's biggest extermination camp. The survivors like them helped our generation to gain a better understanding of the meaning and value of life.

That night Joshua received a phone call from the museum receptionist, telling him that she had found the records of Yura.

## 9

Joshua and I sat in the reception room for visitors who were tracking down victims or survivors. Thousands of people had succeeded in looking for clues of their family members or relatives who were killed in the camp. Probably due to the German personality trait of a mechanical sense of duty, the Nazis kept detail records for every prisoner who came to the camp before 1943, including age, weight, colors of eyes and hair, and even the number of decayed teeth in the mouth.

The receptionist showed us a bust photo picture of a young inmate on her computer screen.

She wore a stripe unisex uniform, with a head scarf of the same material over her shaved head. When the photo was zoomed in, we saw a pair of charming but desperate eyes before us. Joshua took out the photo in his wallet and compared it with the one on the computer screen. They were the same person, and it was Yura. She was smiling in one but looked depressed in the other. The caption below the photo: Yura, Registration on 18 December 1941.

Taken away from her home in Strasbourg, Yura was forever separated from her family. She was led into a windowless cattle train. The door of the car was opened for a split second only when food had to be sent in, but only with a space that a bag of rye bread and a barrel of water could come in. People in the car were not able to see each other's face clearly, but under the pressure of starvation they struggled by instinct for the bread with loud noises. Children cried when they were knocked down, and women's long hair was torn out by the roots. The air was filled with an overpowering stench, because there was no toilet in the car. Yura didn't know how long they traveled, but she knew she had just one piece of bread on the way. However, she still had her violin with her when they arrived at Auschwitz. She had used the same instrument since she learned to play it at the age of eight. It had simply been integrated into her life.

With much noise, her train pulled in at the end of the route of the Death March in front of Camp II. When the inmates got off, they were required to stand in two lines, a female line and a male line. Each of them was instructed on which camp to go to after a physical examination.

An officer with an opaque face came over to Yura. In his hand was a whip, with the cord wound around the stock. Yura had no idea whether it was for prisoners or horses in the camp. Opaque Face looked at Yura and then touched her violin with his whip. "You play the violin? Do you love Johannes Brahms?"

Yura nodded in fear, hoping she had answered both of his questions. The officer forced a smile. "That's very good. You go to the orchestra. I love Brahms."

This aroused Yura's desire for freedom. She had never expected that the camp managed an

orchestra. She wondered whether that was what
the she saw over the gate meant: Arbeit Marcht
Frei. She may be set free if the officer was satisfied
with her Brahms, she thought. The seventeen-year-
old Yura was too naïve and inexperienced in life
to imagine how horrible the hell of the Nazi camp
would be.

Like other women inmates, Yura was shaved
and was given a stripe uniform, but she didn't have
to do slave labor. Along with more than twenty
fellow prisoner musicians, she prepared for their
performances in a wooden house. They played
Johannes Brahms, Claude Debussy, Ludwig van
Beethoven, or any music that Opaque Face selected.
From time to time, Opaque Face brought old music
for the musicians to play. Believing that a lover of
music may have a kind heart, Yura hoped that the
musicians may be dealt with leniently.

The violinist in the camp was a man in his
fifties and used to be the concertmaster in the
Vienna Philharmonic. He was whipped by Opaque
Face whenever he hit a clinker, so he seemed to be
frightened before the office. Yura later learned that
Opaque Face had been a violinist before the war

and he lost much of one of his fingers in a battle. He could no longer draw the bow of a violin cross the strings properly, but he could use a whip. That was why he wore a glove all year round.

Opaque Face was somewhat kinder to Yura. When he came to the wooden house, he often required her to play a solo violin piece. When she finished, he would hit his boots with his whip handle, which served as a ripple of his applause. When the music put him on a jovial mood, he would also throw some biscuits or candy to her, which reminded Yura of the animals in a circus. Yura began to realize that in the hell on earth humanity had been lost on the guards. All that an inmate hoped for was to be lucky enough to survive as long as possible, even in a way that animals do. Human dignity was way beyond their expectation.

One day before Easter, Opaque Face came and told the musicians that they could select a set of clothes and a pair of shoes in the warehouse for the holiday performance for German officers and soldiers. They felt much relieved. The violinist from Vienna had been suffering from recurrent bouts of fever. He would have been gassed if he had been in the labor camp. As the first chair violinist in the orchestra, he knew he would at least survive till Easter, because the officer loved music.

Clothes piled high in the warehouse, but their owners must have been executed. Before they were gassed, the inmates were stripped of their clothes, shoes, jewelry, and glasses, which were placed according to their category. Yura chose for herself a white seersucker V-neck dress with red dots that had ruffles at the neck and along the hem. The dress was beautiful and rather new, and it seemed that the owner hadn't worn it much before she was killed. She must have been about my age, Yura thought. With the dress on, Yura found tears streaming down her cheeks. She believed she continued the life of the dress owner.

Every musician went all out at the performance. The first chair violinist finished without a single wrong note, though he had a splitting headache because of the fever. Every one of them knew that their life depended on the attitude of Opaque Face.

Several Jewish inmates were selected to be cooks and waiters during the performance, because some of them had run restaurants before they were captured. Like the musicians, all of them attempted to make best use of their unique skills, because they too knew that they had to rely on the needs of the Germans to continue to live.

The orchestra was instructed by Opaque Face to prepare for the Christmas performance in late December of 1944. A fire in a stove made of stones was started at a corner of the house, as a favor bestowed by Opaque Face. The musicians were allowed to warm themselves when they found it hard for them to continue with their stiff fingers.

Opaque Face came to the wooden house again. When the Brahms music was over, all of a sudden he exploded with anger, beating the instruments with his whip violently. He roared like a lion. "Put your instruments into the fire, Jewish pigs! You do not deserve to be called musicians."

A deathly silence hung over the room. It was the cold winter of 1944 and everyone knew what happened. It seemed the distant roll of the Soviet guns could be heard. With her arms around her violin, Yura said: "Officer, we're going to celebrate Christmas, aren't we?"

Opaque Face lashed Yura with his whip and

broke her violin in half under his foot before moving it into the fire with his feet. It was at the night on the same day that Opaque Face led the musicians into the gas chamber. About two months later, Auschwitz was liberated by the Soviet Red Army.

A daily journal kept by Opaque Face is kept in the Auschwitz Museum. It has been translated into several languages. When Joshua and I finished reading it, the receptionist printed Yura's photo and handed it to Joshua. "Sir, go to Exhibition Room 7 in Building 15, Camp 1. Photos of the orchestra are kept there."

Exhibition Room 7 was a small room, with large photos of the orchestra when they were performing. The photos were all in a yellow-brown hue due to their old age and only vague outlines of people could be observed. It seemed they were all men. Joshua and I examined each photo, hoping we could find Yura. We searched the photos again and again, but no one in the pictures looked like a woman. Suddenly a picture taken in the summer of 1943 grabbed my attention when I saw a triangle-shaped head scarf on the head of a prisoner in the back row. In the camp, Nazis shaved off women inmates' heads soon after their arrival, so they had to don a head scarf. The female musician's face was behind the violin on the shoulder of a man before her, but I could see her skirt, socks, and shoes with straps.

"It must be Yura," I found myself almost shouting. Hearing my voice, several visitors behind us stopped to take a look at the picture.

The guide for the room came over and asked me in English: "Are you looking for the files of the musicians? Come along with me."

We followed her to a corridor in the building. On the wall were more than twenty bust photos of prisoners. The photos were so large that they clearly showed their facial expressions.

We stopped before the ninth picture in the second row. It was Yura looking at Joshua and me. She had a scarf over her head, her eyes looked depressed, and her lips were slightly apart, looking as if she had been obsessed with too many questions about the world.

Joshua and I each taped a pink carnation under the picture of Yura. Joshua touched her face and said: "Yura, you have been away for more than sixty years. Today is when you go back home." I spoke to her too, but in my heart. "Yura, it is no longer cold here. People with integrity all over the world are coming with the sunlight of humanity."

# 10

When we left Auschwitz, an unusual heat wave had gripped southern Poland. The old train wobbled along, clanking and rattling over the rails, and I felt as if I was in a steamer over a pan of boiling water. My mind was beginning to shift from the death camp to reality. Joshua, however, had been looking outside the window without a word. He hadn't even touched his water.

In our car was also a group of Jewish high school students, ages fourteen or fifteen. They must be spending their summer holiday traveling around, I thought. Their eyes were red from crying when they went aboard, but now some of them were enjoying their soda and potato chips and others buried their heads in video games. It was easier for them to step out of the shadow of the death camp into the sunlight of reality. I felt somewhat relieved. It is enough for children in their flowering years to learn about what happened in Auschwitz, but it is even essential that they live in peace and harmony, breathing sweet, fresh air and enjoying friendship and love.

Several dozens of German-speaking pupils in a summer camp uniform came into our car at a small station. The young woman teacher approached us and asked if it was OK for the kids to place their bags onto the rack over our head. Joshua and I answered "Yes, of course" and helped her put the bags of all colors in place. When the train started to move again toward Kraków, the teacher took the seat opposite us while mopping the sweat from her brow. She spoke good English and seemed pleased to meet travelers from other cultures.

She told us they were from Bavaria and the pupils were spending their time in a summer camp. With her beautiful dancing eyes looking at us, she said: "It is the decision of the Bavarian government that all pupils need to visit Nazi camps and contact the victims. In this way the children will remember the past and are against the revival of German Nazism." All of a sudden, Joshua stood up and bowed to the teacher, with tears in his eyes.

When saying goodbye to the German teacher and her pupils, I was recalling what a Second World War historian said: the deaths in the massacre were not meaningless sacrifice; what the victims left to the future generations is the most valuable gift for life.

I could see no more tears in Joshua's eyes. He said to me with great resolution: "Yao Yao, I'll persuade Operation: Last Chance that they needn't worry about a Fourth Empire, because an insurmountable barrier has been there for years. The barrier is an impregnable fortress built with the blood of the victims in the Nazi massacre. It is called Auschwitz."

On the plane back to Lyon, Joshua took my hand and held it in his. That was the first time my hand had been held by a man. We were strangers twenty days before, but I knew we would not separate at the airport after we had experienced the death camp with a particular part of our lives. Probably, we would be together for a long time. I turned to Joshua, and I saw the same expectation in his eyes.

"Back in Lyon, we need to go to the tourist agency, to show Anne some pictures we took," I said. Joshua nodded with a smile, holding my hand more firmly.

# Normandy Rainbow

# I

Yang Qingfen pushed the door open and found her home was quiet. But somewhere a long sigh from her daughter was clearly audible. Her daughter had uttered few words since she found out the scores for her college entrance examination, but frequently faced the wall and slowly breathed out a few sighs, each full of bitterness and sadness. This pierced her mother's heart. The daughter had tried her best, but her score had not even qualified her for a second-rate four-year college; she came up short by just seven points. Her score was just sufficient for a junior college. Qingfen did not want her daughter to remain in high school for another year and sit for the college entrance examination again the next year, nor did she wish her daughter to enter a fly-by-night junior college. She determined to find a way to save her daughter's reputation—as well as her own.

Qingfen had intended to leave her daughter undisturbed, but their entire home was just one and half rooms, just 20 square meters. There wasn't even space for an extra tea cup to stand. Since her daughter had most likely heard her come in, Qingfen decided she might just as well make some noise to signal her presence. She went to the kitchen, cut open a water melon, removed the red pulp into a porcelain bowl and then called her daughter with an intentionally light and pleasant tone, "Sining, come and enjoy the watermelon. Iced. Couldn't be sweeter."

The daughter sat opposite her mother on a small stool, eating the watermelon, with a trace of tears on the corners of her eyes. Once again there was silence in the kitchen, with only slight noises of a ladle touching a porcelain bowl. The daughter, eyes on the empty bowl, whispered, "Mom, Zhuzhu is going to college in Australia. She went to apply for the visa today." Zhuzhu was Sining's best friend. They had been in the same class since primary school. Zhuzhu's college entrance exam result hadn't been very good either. Her score just reached the bottom line for the admission into a second-rate four-year college, but not enough for a competitive major. It was not unlike going to a vegetable market near nightfall, where you could only get the rejected vegetables. Both of Zhuzhu's parents were public servants in the government and fairly wealthy. They did not want to see their daughter suffer humiliation. So they decided to send Zhuzhu abroad for her college education.

Hearing her daughter's comment, Qingfen's eyes brightened up, "Hey, Sining, why haven't we come up with a plan like that? You could go abroad for your college education like Zhuzhu."

"Mom, are you kidding? The cost for overseas study amounts to at least one or even two hundred thousand yuan a year. The little salary you earn as a community hospital nurse is barely enough to keep me alive." A faint hope that glimmered in her eyes vanished instantly. She lowered her head again, not wanting her mother to see the tears in her eyes.

The expression in her daughter's eyes was just like her father's. Several years before, as her sick husband lay dying in her arms, struggling with sleeplessness every night because of the pain, a hope for life would glimmer in his eyes whenever he heard his wife say, "You'll get better." Qingfen had not been able to save her husband's life, but at that moment, she silently swore to her husband that she would never let that expression of hopelessness appear in her daughter's eyes.

The next day Qingfen was off duty. She had hoped to talk about the possibility of an overseas study plan, but her daughter went to help Zhuzhu to buy a laptop computer. As she had left, she said, "Mom, I know I am a child of a single parent. So I don't expect to have the kind of good fortune Zhuzhu may have. Forget about it."

Her daughter's words had stung Qingfen deeply. What was meant by good fortune or bad fortune? Wasn't it just a matter of money? If she was willing to spend money for Sining, she could go abroad like Zhuzhu and choose a university and a major she liked. When she came back for a job, she would be a returning overseas student, with unlimited promise. Her husband used to tell her that a girl should be brought up in an economically indulgent manner so that she could develop a noble and elegant manner. What Qingfen understood by "indulgent" was never to resist spending money on her daughter, no matter the personal cost.

Qingfen's husband had left only eighty thousand yuan with her and her daughter. The money had originally been intended for her husband's liver transplant operation, but he died before there was time for his operation. After his death, someone consoled her by saying, "That was because your husband loved you and your daughter so dearly and wanted to save money for the family. If he had had the operation and couldn't be saved, wouldn't that have been a loss of both life and money?" Since then Qingfen had never touched that passbook with its burgundy cover. The money in it was an exchange of her husband's life and it could only be spent on their daughter for the most important reason, for her daughter was the extension of her husband's life.

Qingfen stood before her husband's portrait in silence for a while. She then wiped away her tears and put the passbook into her bag, believing that her husband would have agreed to this idea: paving the way to a beautiful future for their daughter. Diagonally opposite the community hospital where

Qingfen worked was Huaxia University. Outside the campus walls, there were five or six overseas study agencies. Every year after the release of the results of the college entrance examination, these agencies were as busy as market-places, teeming with parents and youngsters. The agency Qingfen chose had the same name as the university itself. This name increased her sense of security. With the same name as the university, it should, after all, be more reliable.

The walls of the agency were fully occupied by colorful advertisements for overseas studies. Qingfen's eyes started searching for the information about Australia. Zhuzhu was going to Australia, so Qingfen should do nothing less than that. She would raise her daughter to Zhuzhu's height even on her own delicate shoulders.

"Hello, Madam! Would you like to send your child for overseas studies? Which country do you have in mind? How about having me as your counselor?" A girl in a black suit and with a work card dangling from her neck came to greet her. With a broad smile, she ushered Qingfen into a small compartment partitioned by screens. There was a round glass table with several upholstered chairs.

Qingfen's nervousness was eased with the girl's smile. She took a look at the girl's name card on her chest and asked timidly, "Miss Ye, what's the cost of getting a university education in Australia?" Qingfen pressed her bag tight on her belly as she spoke, as if the passbook in the bag could boost her courage. Miss Ye noticed her movement. A person with a modest financial background lacks confidence anywhere.

Miss Ye was still smiling, "Madam, is your child a boy or girl? Any exam result for TOFEL, IELTS, Intermediate Interpreting, and College English Test Band 4 or Band 6? The cost for the overseas study varies with different universities in different countries."

Except for the fact that she had a daughter, Qingfen had no answers to the other questions. After a moment of hesitation, she went on to say, "My child lost her dad, and I couldn't help in her studies. So her college entrance examination result is not quite satisfactory and she didn't reach the minimum for a second-rate four-year college.

Otherwise, we would never have thought of going abroad to attend college." With these words, she lowered her head as if her daughter's failure in the exam was her own fault.

"Madam, never mind. We the overseas study agency earn our living by doing this. With our varnish on the application package, the majority of the kids get admitted to foreign universities. Next time, please bring your daughter here so that I can give her some advice in person." Miss Ye handed her business card to Qingfen, confident that clients like her came back again.

## II

Sining had never expected her mother to be so determined to send her abroad for her college education. The world in her eyes had turned completely gray immediately after the setback in the matriculation exams. Now her mother presented the card from the overseas study agent in front of her and rekindled her hope. Sining opened her arms around her mother's thin and weak figure and sobbed, "Mom, are you really going to send me abroad? You are amazing."

At this, tears came to Qingfen's eyes. She put the passbook in her daughter's hand, "You should thank your Dad. He left you the money." Sining, passbook in hand, murmured before her father's portrait, "Dad, don't worry, I'll work hard at college and take good care of Mom in the future, I promise." The next day, Qingfen brought Sining to the Huaxia Overseas Studies Agency. Miss Ye greeted them like an old friend and led them to a small room for a consultation. Sining said with a flushed face, "My English is not good and I haven't got any certificate for English exams. Will that be a problem for my application to study abroad?"

Miss Ye put her hands on Sining's shoulders and consoled her like an older sister, "Little Sister, don't worry. Even if you have never learned any foreign language, we can still figure out ways to send you overseas and make your dream of studying abroad come true." She then produced a stack of documents about foreign schools from a file folder. Mostly they were in foreign languages, but a few had Chinese translations. All the documents had eye-catching colored pictures.

"Dear Madam and Little Sister, look, these are the materials about the preparatory school in France. You'll just study French there. The entrance hurdle is quite low, and just a high school graduation certificate from China will do. The tuition for the preparatory school may be a little bit expensive, but once you enter a public university one year later, everything will be OK, with free tuition and only a small registration fee. So the French government will pay Little Sister's tuition and make her a college graduate. Besides, Little Sister is so beautiful and when she is in France for education, she can meet more French girls and that will surely make her more graceful and elegant. That will help her find a husband of a higher notch in future." When Miss Ye was saying this, she was watching the reaction from mother and daughter. Even though the last few sentences were only half serious, she still believed that her judgment of this family's economic situation and her reading of the girl's thoughts couldn't be too far wrong.

As could be expected, when Qingfen learned that tuition was free at all the French public universities, she was surprised with joy and sat dumbfounded with her mouth wide open. She stared at Miss Ye for quite a while before she could utter, "Really? How could there be such a place on earth?"

In the brochures, Sining found a group of boys and girls of different backgrounds picnicking on the grass. Behind them, hidden in the green trees were school buildings like little houses found in fairy tales. In Sining's mind, France was a country renowned for perfume, wine, fashionable dress and beautiful ladies. If she could get to France, Zhuzhu's Australia, where the air was full of the rank odor of sheep and cattle, would pale in significance. She was very interested and said to her mother, "Mom, let's decide on France. Miss Ye can't be wrong." What was in Sining's mind at this moment was how to make show off of her romantic idea of France to Zhuzhu.

Qingfen gave the agency 5,000 yuan as a down payment and Miss Ye saw the two off at the door, "Madam and Little Sister, please rest assured, we'll prepare your passport, visa, airplane ticket, letter of admission, and even lodging in France. Little Sister

will only need to bring a suitcase to go to college."
Qingfen thanked Miss Ye again and again and then
said, "Dear Miss Ye, we'll count on you, we'll count
on you for that. We look forward to the good news."

Hardly had Sining gone out of the agency
when she eagerly sent Zhuzhu a text message. It had
been the happiest day since the publicizing of the
college entrance exam result.

In the month to follow, Miss Ye frequently
called Qingfen and Sining, telling them to pay for
a next service or to fill out some forms. Each time
after they saw Miss Ye, the figure in the passbook
dwindled a little bit. But Qingfen's worries could
always be relieved after Miss Ye reported her
progress. Sining had already been daydreaming
about her trip to romantic France and the cost
for overseas study was of no concern to her.
Fortunately, at the end of the process, she still had
15,000 yuan in her passbook. Qingfen breathed a
long sigh of relief when she received her daughter's
passport with the visa and the letter of admission.

Miss Ye treated them honestly. She copied and
kept the invoices and receipts for the costs of the
whole overseas study application process, where she

represented Sining, and gave all the original invoices and receipts to Qingfen. Miss Ye said, "Madam, our company abides by rules and regulations. You can see our company has only charged you 1,000 yuan as commission for my service of more than a month for Little Sister. It was almost like voluntary work for our clients."

Remembering that she had suspected that the agent might stealthily take rebate on the clients, and hearing what Miss Ye had just said, Qingfen felt rather apologetic at heart. Teeth gritted, she produced two hundred yuan from her bag and put it into Miss Ye's hand. Miss Ye pushed Qingfen's arm aside, "Madam, are you kidding? If I did do anything to help Little Sister to realize her dream of going to college abroad, I will be more than happy. If you really tip me, the tip will cost me my 'rice bowl.' Our company stipulates that we should not accept our clients' favors without the company's consent."

Qingfen went directly to the bank from the agency and converted the 15,000 yuan that remained in the passbook into euros so that her daughter could bring that with her. Feeling her mother's affection in each the bank note, Sining burst into tears, "Mom, I'm using up all our money, what can you count on in the future?"

Qingfen wiped the tears off her daughter's face, "Silly girl, I have my monthly salary, don't worry. If you can learn French well enough to qualify for a public university, I'll only have to pay your living expenses. It won't be a heavy burden." Qingfen tried very hard to force an air of ease and relief, but her heart was sinking into a dark hole. She knew very well that her monthly salary was no more than 3,000 yuan and that could barely make ends meet for them in Shanghai. How could she manage to pay the costs of Sining's overseas study in the years to follow in France? Miss Ye had given her a piece of advice on how to handle the problem, but she wouldn't let her daughter know about it at the moment. She would make sure that her daughter would set her feet on French soil free from care and anxiety. As a widowed mother, life had made Qingfen's nerves extremely tough. Whatever she herself could shoulder, she would never let her daughter share the burden.

# III

As Sining stepped out of the Customs of Paris Charles de Gaulle Airport in Paris, she saw a middle-aged Chinese man holding high a cardboard sign with "Miss Liu Sining from Shanghai" in seven big Chinese characters. The man introduced himself to Sining, "I'm Chen Lunian, vice-principal of Quimper French Language School." Standing beside him were a few Chinese students about Sining's age, who seemed to have just arrived in Paris by other flights.

"Mr. Chen, are you going to show us around Paris very soon? Are we going to see the Eiffel Tower first?" Sining asked eagerly.

Chen Lunian smiled with a shake of his head and said, "Liu Sining, you'd better understand that you are here in France to study, not for sight-seeing. We'll set off for Quimper in no time."

Disappointment appeared on the faces of Sining and the other boys and girls, and they dragged their suitcases along after Lunian. For most of them, this was the first time abroad and away from their parents and they couldn't even speak French. Given this, hardly anyone dared to say no to Lunian's arrangements. Sining couldn't even shoot a glance at the Parisian sky, for the railway station was just at the underground level of the Airport, and they didn't need to get out to get on their train.

It was only the beginning of October and the bleak autumn wind had already scattered yellow leaves over the whole of Quimper, a well-known city in Normandy in northwestern France. By midday, their train arrived at Quimper station. Lunian went to fetch a van from the parking lot and drove this group of Chinese kids and their luggage to the French Language School.

Sining didn't find any pretty fairy-tale huts or green lawns. Instead, she saw a three-storied building with mottled exterior walls and wooden shutters where paint had completely peeled off. It stood there like a weather-beaten old man with worn rags loosely draped over his shoulders, hunching his back to greet Sining and her fellow students.

"This is Quimper French Language School. Please get yourselves familiar with the whereabouts now, for I cannot pick you up for school every day in the future. But it is fortunate that none of your lodgings is far away from here," Lunian said.

A boy named Jianjian drew a deep breath and said with an air of contempt, "Principal Chen, we are not refugees begging for a living. The study-abroad agents said the French Language School had first-class facilities. But look at this school. It should have been demolished by a bulldozer long ago. It's nothing but a shack!"

Jianjian's words were followed by noises of agreement from the rest of the students. Sining brought out the study-abroad brochure she had brought from Shanghai and handed it over to Lunian, "Mr. Chen, where are the bijou villas like the ones shown in this picture? Where are the gardens and lawns?"

With an embarrassed smile, Lunian replied, "Remember, this is France. In the Frenchmen's eyes, the older something is, the more valuable it is. This building has withstood World War II and bears historical significance. You ought to take it as fortunate to study in it."

"Fortunate? Our parents spent several hundred

thousand for our study in France, but not for us to live in a dilapidated shed," Jianjian objected, his face red, like a pugnacious cockerel.

"Right, if this wreck is used as a school building, what if an accident happens?" Two girls behind Jianjian muttered.

Sining was thinking of the savings account passbook that her mother had shown her. The money deposited in it was almost an exchange for her father's life. Quite a sum must have been swindled in this joint scheme by the study-abroad agency and Lunian. Suddenly, sadness overwhelmed her and she squatted down by her suitcase and started crying.

An indiscernible panic passed over Lunian's face. This group of kids all came from big cities and had quick minds. They were not as easily deceived as he had expected. Realizing this, Lunian changed his expression and gently tried to pacify them, "Come on, everybody, if you hate having classes here, we can talk more about it later. But it's so late today, and I'll have to send you each to your individual lodging. You don't want to stand here for the night, do you?"

After the long journey, these young boys and girls were already exhausted. Lunian's words reminded them that now, so far away from their parents and in an alien environment, they could not act willfully, like spoiled children. Jianjian gradually calmed down and Sining wiped away her tears. All the boys and girls got into the van with Lunian, like a helpless flock of lambs being driven into a sheepfold by the shepherd.

Lunian parked the van in front of a two-storied building with a yard. Before the van doors were opened, several enormous dogs barked wildly at the van, pressing their front pawns against the van windows. Sining was frightened into loud screams. Then an old woman came out and called them off. The savage dogs walked away obediently with their tails wagging. Lunian told Sining to get out of the van and then he said to the old lady, "Madame Sophie, this is your new tenant Liu Sining."

Sining greeted the old lady in the French she had just learned, "Bonjour, Madame." Madame Sophie smiled, "Bonsoir, mademoiselle." Sining looked embarrassed, realizing that she had got the time expression wrong.

No sooner had Madame Sophie shown Lunian and Sining into the living room on the ground floor than she withdrew her smile. There was a printed leasing contract on the tea table next to the sofa. Madame Sophie asked Lunian to interpret for her, "Today is October 4th. The tenant must pay 200 euros in rent for a full month. Then on each fourth day of each month, the monthly rent will be paid."

Sining stared blankly at Madame Sophie, wondering why the tens of thousands of yuan they had paid should not have covered the 200 euros of rent for the first month since Miss Ye of the Shanghai agency repeatedly claimed that they had arranged everything for her. Sining had to walk to the corner of the living room, lift her coat and with a big effort, tear open a small, tightly sewn pocket on the lower part of her undergarment. The 1,500 euro cash her mother had given her was there. Sining took out two green one-hundred euro bills and handed them to Madame Sophie. She then had to sign her name where the old lady indicated on the leasing contract before she was entitled to enter her temporary shelter—a small room, barely twelve square meters.

In the room was a single bed, near the head of which were an old-fashioned desk with carved patterns and an upholstered chair of the same carved patterns. Opposite them were a row of cupboards out of which a musty smell burst when the doors were pulled open. Sining sat on the side of the bed and looked around. All of a sudden, she felt enclosed by an indescribable sense of loneliness. She began to feel homesick after a mere twenty hours away from Shanghai. It was the time for her mother to knock off and go home. Soon the delicious smell of food would overflow from the kitchen. But at that moment here in France, no one asked if she was hungry or not. Madame Sophie was busy feeding her dogs.

Sining's eyes were wet again. She took out her cell phone and sent a text message to her mother, "Mom, I've safely arrived at Quimper and settled down. Please don't worry about me." In about just two minutes, she received her mother's reply, "Baby, take good care of yourself and focus your attention on your studies. Mom will always be backing you up." Sining couldn't help bursting into tears, wondering how her mother was getting along since she had left Shanghai. Her mother could not have imagined that her daughter was going hungry with tearful eyes in a strange old woman's home.

## IV

In the corridor of the French Language School, Sining saw the sunny handsome Jianjian coming her way. He was enjoying music from the MP3 plugs in his ears and shaking his head this way and that. In this alien place, Jianjian was the person Sining was most familiar with. When Jianjian saw Sining, he pulled out his earphones and pointed to a classroom at his back with his thumb, "Here's the classroom for us complete beginners. The teacher isn't here yet. I'll hang around outside for a while." This said, he plugged in his earphone again and shook himself away.

There were about twenty students in the beginner's class and they were all Chinese. Since there was no language barrier between them, they just clustered together in twos and threes, chatting and laughing. Sining seemed to feel she was back in

Shanghai, for this was just like a scene of her high school classroom.

A girl with narrow eyes waved to Sining, "Liu Sining, come here, would you like some chips? French chips really are more delicious than the Chinese ones."

Sining now recognized her. She was one of the students Chen Lunian picked up at the airport a few days before. She was a little embarrassed, because the girl could call her by name and treat her to chips, but she didn't know the girl's name yet. Fortunately, Jianjian came back into the classroom at that moment. Following the delicious smell of the chips, he went directly to the desk and picked some up and threw them into his mouth, saying, "Mi Lala, you are so smart. Where did you buy these chips? I'll go and get some in a while."

Lala suddenly brightened up and her eyes twinkled, "Well, our school looks shabby, but shopping is quite convenient. I have already walked around. You'll find a Carrefour supermarket after ten minutes if you take a shortcut from the side gate of our school. There are all kinds of shops there, even an Internet café."

Sining couldn't imagine how Lala already knew the neighborhood here so well. Sining was far more timid. She couldn't even find a bakery because she couldn't communicate with the landlady in French. Sining immediately said to Lala, "If you go to the supermarket, please bring me there, too. I need to do shopping to cook for myself."

Lala was astounded, "Cook for yourself? My goodness! Miss Liu is so smart and able."

Jianjian took up, "Cooking? If I had to cook for myself, I would never have come abroad. Let's go to a fast food restaurant in a while. My treat."

Lala patted Jianjian on the back in great joy, "Of course, that should be on a man."

The whole class waited for about half of the class hour before the secretary came to the classroom and announced, "Your French teacher cannot come for class due to personal business, please go back." The secretary then just turned away and left, not even bothering to give an explanation or apology. The school just took it for granted; probably because this had happened frequently in this school.

The class quieted down, but in just a few

seconds, Lala started to shout for joy, "Hurrah, our teacher has given us a leave. Let's go shopping." Sining was a little disappointed and pulled at Lala's coat, "Why are you so happy about our teacher's absence? We have already paid so much in tuition."

Lala twitched her mouth and came to whisper to Sining, "Do you really want to be a straight-A student? Everybody knows this kind of fly-by-night schools collude with overseas study agencies to fool people for money. Otherwise, how would it be so easy for you and me to get our visas?"

Sining, remembering her mother's expectant eyes, was extremely anxious, "But what if we do not work hard on the year-long preparatory French courses and cannot get admitted to a public university?"

Impatience appeared on Lala's face, "Don't we have a whole year? Let's just muddle along. Now, tell me whether you want to go to Carrefour or not. If you don't, I'll just go without you."

Sining was relieved to be shopping in the supermarket with Lala and Jianjian. She hadn't had a decent meal for several days. So her eyes were stuck on the food racks. Two euros for a bundle of three carrots, 15 euros for 200 grams of boxed pork, 8 euros for 4 croissants in a bag ... As Sining was looking at the price tags for the food and quickly calculating prices in yuan, her heart was beating quickly. Food here was so expensive that she could hardly believe her eyes. With these kinds of living expenses, the money she had brought from Shanghai could hardly last for three months. But Sining would have to bring some food back today, for she should at least keep herself alive. Sining bought a carton of milk for one euro. Baguettes were comparatively inexpensive, and she also chose the cheapest eggs among many varieties—30 for 7 euros. In fact, on the food shelf, there were also the Danone yogurt and black chocolate that Sining loved. They were just common daily foods in Shanghai, but now here they were upgraded to the category of luxuries and she had to fight back her desire for them.

Lala and Jianjian pushed their shopping carts to the cashiers and waited for Sining there. Their carts were full, and the shopping basket in Sining's hand looked measly. Lala asked Sining in great bewilderment, "Why not buy more? It's not all that near to where you live."

Sining flushed with embarrassment, but she couldn't tell her the true cause. So she lowered her head and murmured, "If I buy more, I'm afraid they might be too heavy for me."

Lala burst into laughter and then simple-mindedly began to console Sining, "Please rest assured. I'll buy a car in a few days and I'll take however much you buy to your home."

Sining was flabbergasted at Lala's words, for while she even had to grudge herself yogurt and chocolates, Lala was about to buy a car in France. How could she be so rich?

Jianjian kept his promise and insisted on treating Lala and Sining to a meal. He chose a fast food restaurant with a Brittany seafood theme next to the supermarket and ordered three prawn set meals, each for 25 euros, without even a pause.

Believing that Jianjian must have gone out of his mind, Sining desperately pulled his arms, "If you really wish to treat us, just buy us McDonald's food or pizza. This restaurant is too expensive."

Jianjian released himself from Sining's hands, "Miss Liu, you are not serious! You might as well starve to death if you think food in this place is too expensive."

Lala started to mediate, "Let Jianjian treat us here. Let him show off. I can treat him later on."

The owner of the restaurant was around fifty years old and was greeting guests respectfully at the door. After groups and groups of Chinese students came to Quimper, their extravagant expenses spurred the economic development of a large part of the area and the service industry got the most benefits.

Jianjian was very satisfied with the owner's service and after the meal generously left the change as a tip in an almost pompous manner. Sining shot a glance at the change and found they were four two-euro coins.

As they were leaving the restaurant, Lala received a call from her father in China, urgently asking her when she would be buying a car. Lala was a bit impatient, "I have to wait for a few days to decide. There are only Renault and Peugeot car dealers. Probably I'll have to go to Paris to buy a BMW."

That day when Sining got home, Madame

Sophie was sitting in the living room, waiting for her. "Miss Liu, the lease contract does not include water, electricity and gas bills. We share this room, so isn't it reasonable for you to pay half of the cost? Please pay me 30 more euros."

Sining wondered why she should pay half of the cost, since she was there no more than a few days. But her French wasn't very good and she couldn't express her concern. So she went into her own room without saying a word and closed the door with a big bang.

But Madame Sophie was not a person to be so easily dealt with. She came and knocked on the door, "Miss, if you don't pay half of the bills, you must move out. So many Chinese students come to Quimper, they will be lining up to rent my room."

Sining did not open the door but let herself calm down. It was not Shanghai here and her mother was not with her. So even if Madame Sophie was not reasonable at all in her demands, she was at least providing shelter for Sining. A tenant like Sining did not have much power to bargain with the landlady. If only she were as rich as Lala! If that were true, she would immediately pick up her baggage, leave the room and look for better housing. Then she could teach that old lady a good lesson. But she simply couldn't do it. Sining tore open a pocket tightly attached to her underwear and with great care counted out 30 euros. She then put them on the tea table in the living room.

Madame Sophie was watching TV. She glanced from the corner of her eye and caught every detail. A quick smile of victory flashed across her face.

Winter in Normandy set in extremely early. Snowflakes came flying in the air even in early November. In the whole month since Sining had arrived in France, there had been only twelve days with classes. This French language school did not have a teaching plan involving regular teachers, or even course books. In class, the teacher just gave out some handouts at random, much of the content of which could be found in a French-Chinese dictionary. When a teacher could not come to teach, Lunian himself would teach instead, or just went and found a high school student to fiddle away a few hours. Sining and the other Chinese students were treated as if they were a herd of animals the school raised and only needed a man to guard the gate of the fence. Sining did not dare to tell her mother the truth lest she should feel anguished over the money they had paid the overseas study agency. But on the other hand, Sining could not stop feeling worried about her chances of going to a French university. She should not squander away the money her father had left and go back to China with nothing accomplished.

Sining constantly revealed to Lala and Jianjian this worry, but Lala showed no concern for what might happen in the future. The school's failure to give classes without so much as an excuse seemed like one long party to Lala. She had already purchased a red BMW and often took her classmates on fun tours. Sining was naturally among those invited.

At Lala and Jianjian's insistence, Sining had gone with them on a sightseeing to Mount-Saint-Michel. On the way there, seeing Sining's distressed look, Jianjian consoled her, "Sining, you really don't have to worry yourself about whether you can go to a public university. To tell you the truth, Lunian gave a hint that as long as we can stay in this French school for a full year, he would guarantee us the admission to a local public university. You should know that the Chinese students are the God of Fortune for the Normandy area and the local French people hope that we stay here as long as possible. What benefit can they get if we cannot go to college here?"

Sining could hardly believe Jianjian's words, so she turned to Lala. Lala nodded her head with strong certitude, "Now you can rest assured that you and I will have a French university diploma in due time."

"Are we going to return to China with a fake diploma?" Sining wondered aloud.

"Who knows? Do you think fake diplomas only appear in China? So naive!" Jianjian teased.

"I didn't have the intention of studying abroad, but my Dad and Mom thought that if they did not put me abroad for a while, they would lose their reputation. So I'll have to idle away a few years in France. When I return, whatever diploma will do as a result of my stay here." Lala explained.

Sining's eyebrows knitted, "My mother had expected me to be a 'returned overseas student' and get a good job and help our family. If we get a diploma by crooked means and go back to China, our employers might see our true colors."

Jianjian became impatient, "Sining, you live like an old woman, always wishing to make arrangements for your whole life. Isn't that a burden? Take it easy, please. If you cannot find a good job when you are back in Shanghai, I'll ask Papa to help you get one."

Sining envied Lala and Jianjian from the bottom of her heart. Their parents were wealthy and influential, but they could not understand how Sining felt. That evening, Sining sent a text message to pour out her worries and concerns to her good friend Zhuzhu, who was far away in Australia. But Zhuzhu's reply seemed irrelevant, "The outside world is wonderful. You'll be always happy if you have money with you."

# V

Qingfen came to Miss Ye again. After she received her daughter's phone call, she was sleepless all night and early the next morning she came to wait at the door of the overseas study agency. Qingfen asked

Miss Ye, "Didn't you say that the sixty thousand yuan would definitely cover my daughter's fees and expenses for the first whole year in France? Why did my little girl ask for money after only two months?" Miss Ye was still smiling with all ears, "Madam Yang, we are overseas study agency, when we said the costs for a year, we meant the tuition, not including living expenses. If you don't believe me, you can go and carefully check the agreement. It says it in black and white. How could sixty thousand be enough? Besides, kids today are in the habit of spending money extravagantly. Probably six hundred thousand is not even very much for them." Miss Ye answered her with such an honest and reasonable manner that even she made Qingfen feel embarrassed.

On the phone, Sining gave her mother a detailed list of living expenses and said unequivocally that if Mother could not deposit 500 euros each month, she would have to come back to China. Her daughter's sobbing voice stung her mother's nerves so much that Qingfen decided to cross the Rubicon—she decided to sell their home.

Miss Ye read Qingfen's thoughts and tactfully

encouraged her, "Madam Yang, so many parents sell their home for their children's overseas study. We the overseas study agencies call that transfer of assets. No doubt, your apartment is your property, but providing a better education for your child is also a form of investment, and the returns of this investment is inestimable. You sell your old apartment for your daughter's education now, but she might purchase you a big house in return some day." Even without Miss Ye's words, Qingfen was still very clear about her own economic situation. If she really wanted her daughter to join the army of overseas study, she could do nothing but sell their apartment. After saying goodbye to Miss Ye, Qingfen went directly home for the property ownership certificate.

This apartment had been part of governmental housing. It had been allocated to Qingfen's husband by his employer for his family to live in. Later on, they acquired the property rights by paying over ten thousand yuan. From the drawer of their desk, Qingfen took out the property ownership certificate which was wrapped in quite a few layers of plastic bags whose open ends were closed with packing tape. Qingfen remembered her husband's words, "The most valuable thing in our home is this property ownership certificate, take care to keep it from getting damp." When her husband was severely ill, relatives and friends advised Qingfen to sell their home so that her husband could have an operation in Hong Kong. But her husband vehemently disagreed. He knew he was going to die soon and he wanted to keep the shelter for his wife and daughter at any cost.

Qingfen's tears fell on the plastic bag. She promptly wiped them away with her sleeve and looked up at her husband's portrait and said, "I know you will not be happy about selling our apartment, but I have no other choice. Sining needs money to study abroad. I believe you won't grudge me spending money for our daughter." Qingfen put the certificate in her bag and hurried out, without the courage to take another look at her husband's eyes.

There were over ten real estate broker's offices on the street not far away from Qingfen's home. After the government issued the housing price regulatory policies, this business dwindled very fast and visitors were few and far between for each broker. Qingfen stopped in front of quite a grand office. A young man instantly came out to greet her, "Dear Madam, do you want to sell, buy or rent? Please do come in for detailed information." Qingfen sat down before the young man and after a moment of hesitation produced the property ownership certificate from her bag and said, "Sir, please tell me how much I can get if I sell this apartment."

"Madam, my family name is Gu. Please call me Little Gu." With these words, he handed over his business card to Qingfen. He then took a glance at the location and floor space written on the certificate and asked, "Madam, I believe you have heard about the housing price regulatory policies by the government. If not for the urgent need for money, people normally do not sell their homes at this time. Your apartment is not big and you don't have to pay property tax, why do you want to sell it now?"

Qingfen felt that Little Gu was honest in saying that, not like those glib-tongued brokers, so she just told him the truth, "My daughter is now studying abroad and has huge expenses. I cannot support her on my salary, so I have to sell my apartment." With these words, Qingfen's eyes reddened with tears.

Little Gu nodded understandingly, "How unconditional and unselfish parents' love for their children is! Madam, I'll list your apartment right away, but it is hard to say when you can find a buyer. The housing market is sluggish now, and both the sellers and buyers are hesitant about their decisions. We have had no transactions for more than ten days in a row."

Qingfen cashed the only three thousand yuan left in her payroll card into euro and told her daughter not to worry. She would remit enough money to her as scheduled every month. Qingfen didn't want her daughter to know that she had sold their home. She had to do her best to continue to guarantee her daughter's carefree study abroad like the children from wealthy families.

After her apartment was listed, Qingfen went out of her way to stop by at the broker's office almost every day. Of course Little Gu had her cell phone number and would have naturally told her of any progress, so there was no need at all for her to go to the office in person. Every time Little Gu saw Qingfen, he had an air of apology, "Look, Madam, I've already put your apartment in the most conspicuous position, but still no one had made any inquiry about it. If you really want to sell it fast, could you lower the price a little bit?"

Qingfen's heart beat wildly. She knew the housing purchase couldn't be like the bargain in the farmer's market. Any small compromise could mean something like ten thousand yuan less. She had to decline his request very patiently, "Little Gu, I'm not in a hurry. Let's keep waiting for some while. Selling an apartment is no small matter. We'd better be more cautious."

Little Gu was very conscientious about the deal and a week later he told Qingfen that a person wanted to have a look at the apartment on that very day. Qingfen was on duty then, but she didn't want to miss the opportunity, so she made a special shift with a colleague and went back home to wait for the prospective buyer. She tidied up her apartment once again before the prospective buyer came, especially the corners of the kitchen and the bathroom. This was what Little Gu specially told her to give more attention to. He told her that normally, a buyer would inspect those hidden corners carefully.

The prospective buyer Little Gu brought to her home was a man from outside Shanghai. He had been in the flower and plant wholesale business for over ten years in the nearby market and had accumulated some money. So he wished to buy a small second-hand apartment in Shanghai for a permanent settlement. The man was stout and looked like a frank and straightforward person. After he came in, he just took a casual look at the inside facilities and without Qingfen's invitation, seated himself in the couch. He then asked, "Do you have an ash-tray? I'd like to have a smoke."

There was no male living in Qingfen's home. Besides, she worked in the hospital all year round and naturally shunned people around her smoking. But today was different. This man, though a smoker, could be the possible buyer of her apartment and she didn't want any unpleasant occurrence to spoil the possible deal. She instantly went to the kitchen and fetched an enamel plate to use as an ash-tray and seated herself opposite the man. Smoke rose in curves and she was unexpectedly choked to a cough, but she did all she could to maintain the smile on her face.

The man finished his cigarette and then a smile appeared on his face, "Sister, this apartment is not bad. I'll take it at the price listed. But I have one more question, that is, why are you in such a hurry to sell such a neat apartment? Where will you live in the future?"

Qingfen never imagined the buyer could make such a quick decision, without even bothering to bargain. Things went far more smoothly than she had expected. So she told him the honest reason, "My daughter is now studying abroad, but her father died some time ago. My meager salary is not enough to support her if I don't sell my home."

Hearing her words, the man fell into silence and then lit another cigarette, "Then, you don't have to pay your share of the property transaction tax, the agent commission or other fees. They will all be on me."

Little Gu, who had been silent, suddenly asked, "Sir, do you plan to live here yourself or lease it after you purchase it?"

"I'll leave it unoccupied for some while,

because I'm very busy and have to live in my shop in the market place. Next year I'll go and get my wife and children from my hometown and move here."

Little Gu tipped Qingfen a wink and then inquired, "Sir, it's a pity to buy an apartment and leave it unoccupied. You might as well lease it to this lady so that she doesn't have to move out and you can get some rent. Killing two birds with one stone, isn't it?"

The man laughed and patted Little Gu on the shoulder, "Great, young man, you are really a natural estate dealer with a quick mind. No problem, Sister does not have to move out. As for the rent, it's up to you to decide."

## VI

On the 10th day of each month, Sining would invariably receive a remittance of 800 euros in cash sent by her mother from Shanghai. Though she could not purchase without limits on a credit card like Lala and Jianjian, she could still live a carefree life in France. Sining knew her mother's salary

was not high and remembered when in Shanghai,
that at the end of each month, the mother and the
daughter spent time counting the meager money
left in their purse to try and make ends meet.
How could her mother manage to remit such a
large amount of money? Sining didn't give it too
much thought, nor did she want to. Every time she
received money, she would let her mother know by
sending her a text message and her mother's reply
was always the same—that she study hard and not
work part-time to earn money.

Christmas holiday was just around the corner
and the French language school had long before
posted an announcement saying that there would
be a month of holiday for Christmas and New Year.
The Chinese students had got used to the irregular
teaching and began to plan their holiday trip. Lala
was especially enthusiastic and was planning to
take a tour with Jianjian in her red BMW, of the
Netherlands, Belgium and Luxembourg. Lala said
to Sining, "I can take two more companions on the
journey. Which boy do you like, please ask him to
come with us." Naturally, Lala would not let the
riders sit in her BMW for nothing. They would

have to share the gas and tolls. She was copying the French college students' way of sharing expenses.

Sining was a little hesitant. Last time they spent the weekend in Paris in her car it cost her more than 100 euros. If this time she went to the three countries for a big tour, she would spend at least 200 euros and that amount was almost as much as her mother's salary for a whole month. Maybe her mother would not ask how she spent the money, but she herself felt quite uneasy at heart, for since her childhood, she had never spent so much on herself.

Lala became impatient, "Coming or not? Give me a quick answer. More people are queuing up for a ride in my BMW."

Jianjian also added, "In the winter in Normandy, it either rains or snows, without any sign of sunshine. Aren't you afraid of getting depressed?"

Sining was tempted. Facing the landlady's old witchy face for a whole month would definitely drive her mad. So she nodded to Lala, "All right, I'll go. But how much should I pay?" With these words she felt a pang in her heart.

Lala smiled and said casually, "You can just pay 300 euros. If the expenses exceed 300, I'll pay the rest as a treat to you because we are classmates." Lala always treated money lightly.

"300 euros!" Sining could not help crying out. "But all my mother sends me for living expenses each month is 800 euros."

"Liu Sining, how could your mother be so stingy! How can you study abroad on 800 euros a month? Why not just spend much less by staying in China and just eating porridge with pickled vegetables?" Jianjian derided her. For Jianjian and Lala, 800 euros was nothing more than their monthly pocket money.

At this moment, Sining hated herself for hanging out with Lala and Jianjian. Their attitude toward money not only made Sining feel inferior but also weighed heavily on her heart. Sining opened her purse and took out the 800 euros that she had freshly withdrawn from the post office. With teeth gritted, she threw three 100-euro notes to Lala, "Take it. I'll come."

Apart from Sining, Lala did not find another person who wished to travel in her BMW. Someone said to Sining, "Don't be so silly. It will cost you less than 300 euros to do sightseeing in these three countries on the Euroline buses." Sining felt regret about joining Lala and Jianjian. Her act of throwing three 100-euro bills at Lala had been simply out of a fit of pique. She did it to avoid being looked down upon by Lala. But now with a cool head, she realized that it wasn't wise at all of her to be so serious about money matters with Lala, because not everyone in this world had a wealthy entrepreneur as father to support him. But Sining didn't change her mind, for she knew if she went to ask for money back from Lala, she would hear a barrage of mean words from that princess of a wealthy family.

Though it was already winter now, the views on both sides of the highway from Normandy to the Netherlands were still enchanting. Against the gray sky, the boughs and branches where all the leaves had shed looked like a gloomy Chinese brush painting. The fields became yellowish brown. Countless crows perched on the bundles of straw and at the sight of a car they would suddenly flutter their wings for far and beyond.

On the drive, Lala and Jianjian rotated at

the wheel and frequently had close contacts by bending their arms around each other, leaving the comfortable and spacious back seat to Sining. And they didn't seem to mind the presence of a third person behind them. One day, as they drove along Sining kept looking out of the window. If it wasn't for European law stipulating that everyone in the car should wear a seat belt, she would have liked to lie down to avoid Lala and Jianjian's live love show. The cell phone rang and the text message from her mother helped Sining avert her embarrassment. She lowered her head and fiddled with her cell phone: "Honey, how are you getting on? What do you have for your meals these days? Is the money enough for you? Please don't be frugal. Just tell me if you are short of money." Her mother texted her almost every day and always repeated these words. Sining didn't know why, and she had to text back again and again, "Mom, everything is going well with me. It's holiday time now and I'm reviewing my lessons at home. I'm quite well and not short of money. Please don't worry about me." Sining did not dare tell her mother the truth, for her mother would definitely fly into a rage if she knew Sining spent 300 euros for just one excursion with her classmates. Even though her mother loved her so dearly, perhaps she still could not stand her daughter's extravagant behavior. Feeling guilty for not telling her mother the truth, Sining sent one more text message to her mother, "Mom, please have some better food. Do not always buy vegetables at the closing time at the market. Health is of vital importance." When in Shanghai, any sign of her care and attention for her mother would move her mother to tears.

While Sining was texting her mother, Jianjian drove off the ramp and pulled in at the road side. Lala said to Sining with a flushed face, "We are going to relieve ourselves, please take care of the car for a while. You can go after we come back." Sining felt that it was strange for Lala to say this—common sense would have the females going off together. But why had Lala asked her to stay to look after the car? Sining didn't give it another thought. Since the car had been stopped, she just unbuttoned her safety-belt and lay down on the back seats.

More than an hour passed by and the sky gradually dimmed, but Lala and Jianjian hadn't finished. Sining was a bit worried, so she cried at the top of her voice in the direction they had left. Surprising her, Lala and Jianjian jumped out from the bushes about ten meters away from the car. Lala complained with a long face, "Sining, why did you scream so wildly? You aren't going to be eaten by wolves." Seeing their unkempt hair and clothes, Sining instantly understood what had happened. She then flushed and said, "I also want to relieve myself. I cannot hold it any longer."

Sining went to the grass near the bushes and her eyes accidentally hit on a small brightly colored packet. The two overlapping hearts verified her guess just now. Sining kicked at it with the tip of her shoe. Shameless! Bringing this kind of stuff with them! She thought. She was not clear whether she despised or envied Lala. Maybe she was just letting out some of the inner disappointment and depression of a girl of the same age.

## VII

Wang Lianyin always came to collect the rent in person on the last day of a month. The flowers and plants dealer did not seem quite accustomed to using a bank card, probably believing the cash in his hand would make him feel more secure. When he decided to buy Qingfen's apartment, he simply carried over 500,000 yuan in two shopping bags to her, and then signed the property transaction contract.

Qingfen's life in this apartment did not seem to change much except the property owner's name and a monthly rent of 500 yuan. Wang Lianyin meant what he said and allowed Qingfen to continue to live there after she sold the apartment and simply asked for half of the rent for an apartment of a similar condition. He did so not because he had pity for a woman who had lost her husband, but because he couldn't quite get his head around owning the property and being a landlord in a metropolis.

Qingfen had already prepared a bottle of Champion Red yellow wine and some plates of home-made dishes to go with the wine. She was a wise woman. Since Wang Lianyin had bought her apartment for more than 500,000 yuan and become the owner, but did not live in it and asked for less rent, she thought she should at least did something in return for the benefits. Another reason why Qingfen was willing to treat this man was that though he drank and smoked, but when he knew Qingfen worked in a hospital, he only drank a little bit, but held back on his smoking. This kind of self-restraint could be called "well-cultivated" for people of his background.

That day, Lianyin came with a bag of fruits and a pot of purple moth orchids. They were in full bloom and Qingfen loved them. Lianyin said, "At this time of the season, the purple moth orchid is at its best. I know you women love flowers and plants and such, so I just brought a random pot to you. This flower is easy to care for. You'll just need to put it in a cool place and water it every other day." Lianyin obviously was not the romantic urban man who knew how to please women by buying them flowers. His act was just like bringing some local produce when countryside folks go to visit relatives in the cities. Although Lianyin could not rid himself of the rustic manner, Qingfen still felt thrilled the moment she received the flower. This was the first time in her life that a man ever presented her with flowers. Along with her "thank you," her heart, though like still water for a long time, began to flutter wildly in her chest.

Lianyin loved to have dinner face to face with Qingfen. He sipped a little wine, picked up some dishes with his chopsticks while half raising his face with narrowed eyes. He seemed to so enjoy these evenings. Qingfen knew for sure she was a good cook, but just politely said, "Sir, please forgive my bad cooking. I don't know how to make good home dishes, but do help yourself to some."

Lianyin flushed at her words, certainly not because of the alcohol, but because of the unknown sense of inferiority before a Shanghai woman. He waved his hand, "Don't call me 'Sir,' just call me Old Wang. I've had boxed meals for over ten years and have never had such good fortune as today." Lianyin was now Qingfen's landlord and although he had a flower and plant wholesale shop, he didn't have the presumption to see himself a better businessman than Qingfen.

After the meal, Qingfen made a cup of jasmine tea for Lianyin and put an envelope with the rent of 500 yuan beside the tea cup. Lianyin pushed aside the envelope, "You can continue to live in this apartment in future, but I won't charge you any rent. Send more money to your daughter. It's not easy for a child to get along away from home."

"That won't do. No matter how poor I am, I cannot live in your apartment for free. It just wouldn't be right." Qingfen pushed the envelope back toward Lianyin's hand firmly, almost upsetting the cup. She was intent on maintaining her self-esteem.

Lianyin lowered his head, rubbed his hands between his legs and murmured, "The other day I met with Little Gu from the real estate broker's office. He asked me to treat him to a good meal because housing prices are rising every day. So even if I do not take any rent from you, I still have a good bargain on hand. The money you got from your apartment will go day by day. As a man, I cannot shamelessly take advantage of a widow and a fatherless daughter." Lianyin was harsh towards men in business and he always believed that the wins and losses in business totally depended on a businessman's ability. But at this moment, he really didn't have the heart to collect rent from Qingfen.

A sense of gratitude rose up from Qingfen's

heart. This seemingly rustic man did have a loving heart. But she insisted and pushed the envelope back, "If you don't take the rent, I'll move out tomorrow and you cannot expect to have a place to enjoy these homemade Shanghai dishes."

Qingfen soon got the better of Lianyin in this half-joking manner. He put the envelope into his pocket with a little shame and then shook his head, "Qingfen, people always say that Shanghai women are shrewd and cunning. Why are you not like that?" Qingfen raise her hand and slapped Lianyin on the back of his hand, "Nonsense, you non-Shanghainese folks are bad."

That night, Lianyin didn't go back to the flowers and plants wholesale shop. It was the first time he slept in the apartment he had bought. From then Lianyin developed an attachment he hadn't had before to the apartment. Whenever Qingfen was off duty, he would keep her company at home, not even caring about the loss of business. Lianyin just wished for a feeling of home and a good rest after a long tiring day. Ironically, his real home in the countryside, which he had been away from for too long, seemed unreal.

Qingfen struggled with the decision to let Lianyin stay the night. She had no sense how her neighbors would view her behavior. A woman of more than forty couldn't live rashly, like a twenty-year-old girl. However, she soon came to terms with it and felt relived because all the more important and wealthy neighbors had moved out one by one and the old homes were all leased to people from outside of Shanghai. So now there were really no people left in the building knew her history. Some people even took Lianyin for her husband. Qingfen thought better of telling her daughter about the sale of their home. Even if her daughter came back to China for her next summer vacation, it wouldn't cross her mind to verify the property ownership certificate with her mother. But what Qingfen felt sorry about was that it was not quite fair to her husband, because she changed his name on the certificate to another man's name. And what was worse was that she was now cohabitating with the man in the same apartment where her husband once lived. Qingfen put away her husband's portrait, for she dared not look again at her husband's warm and kind eyes. For many years, this pair of eyes had been the spiritual prop for her and her daughter.

There were times when Lianyin did not feel secure while sleeping in this apartment. His son was going to middle school the next year and his wife wanted their son to attend school in Shanghai so that the family could live together. Lianyin had decided to buy a home for their future life in Shanghai. He knew how much he loved Qingfen and the development of their affair was not only the result of mindless pursuit on his side. He had never dared to have any fantasies about his tenant. He felt they were just like strangers on a journey. They would regard their meeting as a predestined fate and would not feel sad when they had to part. Lianyin rarely mentioned his wife and son who remained in his hometown, fearing that would lead to Qingfen taking offense or misunderstanding.

Qingfen now only wished that the money she got from the sale of their home could last until her daughter finished college, then her daughter could find a good job as a returned overseas student, and finally they could even buy a new apartment in Shanghai. Though Miss Ye from the overseas study agency described the future as rosy for those returning from study abroad, Qingfen barely dared to expect her daughter to come back and have the success necessary to buy a villa for them. If her daughter could bring back a decent university degree, that could be counted as worthy of her and her husband's expectation.

# VIII

The weekend before the preparatory program completion exam Sining kept herself rooted in her small room. This exam would determine whether she could successfully go to a public university. During the year she had been abroad, the actual class time had been no more than three months. With the very loose as well as irregular teaching schedule, Sining didn't even have a grasp of the basic rules for conjugating French verbs. The cashiers and clerks frowned at her French when she tried her French while shopping or was at the bank or the post office; they were horrified that their incomparably beautiful French was being spoiled by foreigners. What bothered Sining most was the money her mother sent her every month. It was twice the amount of their combined living expenses in Shanghai. If she would not enter a public university a year later, how would she ever justify herself and face her mother? Besides, her visa was valid for only one year. If she could not go to college, she would have to go back to China. And if that happened, she hated the thought of facing Zhuzhu and her other former high school classmates. These accumulated worries tossed back and forth in her mind and exacerbated her nerves for the forthcoming exam.

Madame Sophie the landlady paced up and down between Sining's door and window, and sometimes made noise on purpose in order to tempt Sining to open the door. Madame had noticed that her tenant had been rather gloomy lately. When she saw the landlady, Sining no longer even greeted her. After supper, she did not watch TV in the living room, but just kept herself tightly shut behind her door. Rigid and even mean as Sophie was, she still kept a close watch over her tenant's daily activities. The girl had traveled thousands of miles to come to France to study and she felt a certain responsibility to ensure that her tenant lived happily.

Sunday evening Sining finally left her room. She saw that the red BMW was parked outside Madame Sophie's courtyard. Lala was wearing hot-pants which were certainly not suitable for the season. She and Jianjian had each had their noses pierced and had silvery rings hanging from their noses. The rings were called "love-bird rings." Lala, fiddling with her tiny ring, asked Sining, "Is it beautiful? Only 150 euros. Why don't you get one, too? A stud near your lip would be super cool."

Sining was frightened and instantly covered her head with her hands as if Lala were going to drag her to have a nail stuck in her mouth. Madame Sophie asked the three youngsters to be seated at a stone table in the garden and brought some freshly made coffee and a plate of biscuits. She was thankful from the bottom of her heart to Lala and Jianjian for coming by with the red BMW, because at least she knew that her young tenant was safe and sound.

Lala suggested Sining come out with them to a

party, but Sining vehemently shook her head, "The exam is just around the corner and I'm so nervous about it. I can't believe you two are going to a party at this time. Are you sure you will get a decent grade?"

Jianjian smiled mysteriously, "Liu Sining, if you go and have fun with us tonight, I'll tell you a top secret. Even if you don't sit for the exam, you'll still be able to enter a public university." As he said these words, Jianjian winked at Lala. Lala took the hint and wrapped her arms around Sining and whispered to her, "Jianjian was not kidding. If you don't go to the party tonight, you'll absolutely regret it. As for entering a public university, you can count on us."

Sining's tortured nerves suddenly relaxed. She didn't have the slightest doubt about the truth of Lala's words. It seemed that there was nothing under the sun that this wealthy girl could not fix. If there really was a shortcut to a public university, why should she turn it down? Her face brightened up with a smile and she went back to her room and changed her clothes. She then jumped into the BMW and drove off with the others. Madame

Sophie returned to collect the coffee cups and discontentedly grumbled, "These kids! They do not even know the most basic manners. How rude they are!"

Sining drank quite a lot at the all-night party and even had her first cigarette, ever. She experienced all sorts of excitement and pleasure that she had never had before. She danced and wiggled and partied with the other kids. At dawn, Sining wanted to go home and dragged Lala and Jianjian to a corner, "You two have to honor your promise. How will you help me to enter a public university?"

"Bring 500 euros to school someday next week and I'll help you fix it," Jianjian said.

"500 euros?" Sining was shocked and sobered up quickly. She cried out in disbelief.

"Why are you screaming?" Lala asked her. "Do you expect someone to help you get such a big deal done without any pay? If you are good enough to get yourself to a public university, that would cost nothing, but are you?" Lala sneered with an air of contempt on her face.

Sining bowed her head. She was not a

confident girl. Since they had hardly had any classes at all since arriving in France, she wasn't remotely confident that she could get into a university—if she missed this chance, there would be no way back for her. So Sining nodded to Lala and Jianjian and said, "All right, 500. It's a deal."

The 800 euros her mother remitted for that month soon ran out and Sining had to make a phone call to Shanghai, "Mom, please send 500 euros to my bank card. Urgent." Her mother was a little surprised and after a moment of silence, agreed. She didn't ask why her daughter needed the money so urgently. This relieved Sining.

She brought the cash to school. Jianjian showed her to the door of Lunian's office, and winked at her and then left. Sining entered the office. Lunian cast a glance in her direction and asked, "Liu Sining, are you also coming to hand in the service fee?"

Sining nodded. She gave him the money and signed her name as guided by Lunian. She had thought that there should be a receipt or something for such a big sum, but Lunian nodded his head toward the door, signaling her to leave.

Sining went out of the office and asked Jianjian in a whisper, "There is no receipt for the 500 euros. He won't deny receiving it, will he?"

Jianjian again showed his signature air of ridicule, "Look, you coward, he is running a business worth hundreds of thousands of yuan. Is a mere 500 euros worthy of his deception?"

Sining now felt reassured. She guessed that Lala and Jianjian must have also taken this shortcut provided by Lunian. With them going before her, she didn't need to worry too much. Sining took part in the French proficiency test any way and got only 7 points. However, the standard matriculation line for the French language for foreign students was 10 points. Sining privately felt that she was rather fortunate. If she hadn't spent those 500 euros, she would have to pack for China.

One month later, Sining, Lala, Jianjian and about ten other Chinese students got admissions notifications from The Normandy Business School. This was a school run by the local chamber of commerce and students only needed to pay 100 euros for registration but were then totally exempt from tuition. Sining immediately called her

mother to tell her this good news and her mother
wept for joy at the other end of the line, "My dear
daughter, honey, thank you for doing this for me.
I'll remit more money as your bonus in a few days."
After hanging up the phone, some sense of shame
rose from her heart. She wanted her mother to be
happy, but didn't want her to know the truth about
her admission.

After her daughter's phone call, Qingfen went
out of her way to buy a box of quality chocolates
and brought it to Miss Ye's office. This act was more
of a show-off than genuine thanks to Miss Ye for
her hard work in helping Sining with her study
abroad project.

When Miss Ye heard The Normandy Business
School, she immediately knew what tricks Chen
Lunian had played. That so-called chamber-of-
commerce-run school was only a community school
in France. It had been intended for the unemployed
and elderly people to get continuing education.
But due to the slow economic development in the
Normandy area, this kind of school began to enroll
foreign students, most of whom were Chinese. The
growing number of foreign students had spurred

local economy. So the government was rather loose in issuing visas. Otherwise, how could youngsters like Sining who could not enter college in China so easily get to study in France? Miss Ye didn't tell Qingfen that The Normandy Business School was neither registered in the French Ministry of Education nor recognized by the Ministry of Education of China. When Sining came back after her graduation, she would just bring back a piece of beautiful waste paper. But at this moment, Miss Ye really didn't have the heart to tell her the truth. She just wanted to let this poor woman be happy for a little longer.

Qingfen made a detailed calculation. If she could deposit half of money in a regular account in the bank at least it would generate some interest. The other half would be deposited in a current account and changed into euros to be remitted to her daughter every month. This money would be enough even if her daughter attended college for four years. After her daughter graduated from college and returned to China and found a good job, she and her daughter could buy a new home by getting a mortgage. Qingfen coveted nothing else for her life as long as she could bring up her daughter to be a successful person.

# IX

Lianyin had been pacing up and down outside the gate for some time, but he still didn't have the guts to go into Qingfen's home. Early that morning, his wife had called him from his hometown, telling him that she would be bring their son and his parents to Shanghai and asking him to tidy up their apartment and add some necessities for daily use. Lianyin was completely stunned by his family's abrupt decision to come to Shanghai. What was worse, his wife spoke with some insinuation, as if her family had caught wind of something indecent about his life in Shanghai. Lianyin should have kept a low profile because quite a few of the helpers in the whole-sale shops and the market were his hometown folks. Secrecy was impossible with so many people around. In this era of quick communication, how could he possibly hide the truth about his activities from his family in the countryside. Some of his hometown folks had even jokingly said they wanted to have a look at their "Shanghainese sister-in-law." Lianyin had never expected that only after a short time in Qingfen's small and comfortable "nest," his wife and all the family would come right to the door on a punitive expedition.

Qingfen was preparing dishes in the kitchen. Cups, plates, bowls and chopsticks had been already set on the table. Even the cork of the wine bottle had been removed. Her daughter had been admitted to a public university as she had wished and Qingfen wanted to celebrate. She had bought Lianyin some good wine for this special occasion and prepared some extra dishes. If it hadn't been for Lianyin's purchase of her apartment, her daughter could not have studied in France without care or anxiety. Now Qingfen poured all her gratitude toward Lianyin into the wine and dishes.

Right after he came in, Lianyin went straight to the balcony to fix the flower pots. Today he brought a pot of primrose and a pot of umbrella papyrus. The array of red and green colors was exceptionally inviting. Still in her happy mood and not even noticing Lianyin's expression, Qingfen said, "Old Wang, my Sining has been admitted into a French public university and I won't have to pay tuition for the four years to come. The French government will pay for her education."

Lianyin sat at the table and raised his cup, "Qingfen, as a mother, your life is not easy, but your daughter is a success and will save you quite a lot of money." After this, Lianyin just helped himself to the wine and dishes silently, not even raising his head, as if Qingfen's joyous event was of no interest to him. After the meal, Lianyin lit a cigarette and the tiny apartment was soon full of smoke.

Qingfen had by now noticed Lianyin's unusual expression, but she herself was in a very happy mood and did not mind his smoking tonight. Furthermore, she was aware of her own status: she was not the owner but the tenant of this apartment.

Lianyin snubbed his cigarette and in a dramatic manner and whispered, "Qingfen, I'm in big trouble now. My wife and child are coming to live in Shanghai. But they don't know that you are living in this apartment." Then his head sank down like an unfaithful man not daring to face the woman that trusted him.

Qingfen suddenly flopped onto the chair. The happiness of the past few days instantly vanished and she couldn't help asking in a trembling voice, "Where will I live?" But she regretted her words the moment she had said them. She had sold her apartment and now had the money in pocket from the sale. Why should she linger on in this home? Just because she had developed an intimate relationship with him it did not give her a right. The sudden shame stung her to sobriety. She tried her uttermost to sit still and said calmly, "Old Wang, don't worry. I'll go to the housing broker to find a room. I'll move out as soon as possible."

Lianyin dared not face Qingfen's eyes but covered his face with both of his hands, "Qingfen, it's too hard on you. I really want to help, but at the moment I can't." Qingfen came up to hold Lianyin's large blue-veined hands, "Old Wang, you've helped me a lot, I'll always cherish that in my heart."

Little Gu was very surprised when he saw Qingfen appear in his office again, "Madam, didn't Old Wang lease that apartment to you? Why are you still looking for a room?"

Qingfen smiled mildly, "His wife and child in

the countryside are coming to live in Shanghai and I have to make room for them as soon as possible." Little Gu said, "Housing prices are very high now, so those who cannot afford to buy their home have to rent and that has made the price increase. At least 1,500 yuan in rent has to be paid for a small apartment like yours."

Qingfen's heart was seized with horror, 1,500 yuan! That would mean half of her salary would go for rent. The price in Shanghai was so high, supporting herself was going to be a problem. So she asked Little Gu, "Could you help me find a cheaper lodging, I'm only by myself now." Little Gu had a warm heart, and Qingfen was his old client, so in the next few days, Little Gu showed her three places for rent. The first two landlords were insistent on the price and wouldn't have Qingfen have their places for even one cent less. The third were an old couple and there was some room for bargaining, but they asked Qingfen to take up some house chores and look after them. That meant that they traded the reduced amount of rent for the money paid to a part-time helper.

Qingfen agreed. As a nurse in a community

hospital for more than twenty years, her job was to attend others. It would matter little for her to take care of two more aged people after work. She might just regard it as a part-time job. Qingfen felt quite sure that if she wanted her daughter to successfully obtain a college degree, she had to make efforts to keep the diminishing figure in her saving account from shrinking. A mother was willing to suffer any hardship for the sake of her daughter.

There were two rooms in the old couple's apartment, one in the southern part, the other in the northern part. The room they leased to Qingfen was the smaller, north-facing room, of only nine square meters, which made it impossible for Qingfen to move in all the stuff from her former apartment. So she had to dispose of most of her things. Lianyin suggested, "You may just as well sell the furniture to me for my family use when they come." Qingfen refused, because she could not stand Lianyin's wife and family using the furniture that she had so prized.

Little Gu asked a few of his buddies to help Qingfen move out. They didn't ask for any money for it, not even a meal. Qingfen knew that Little

Gu didn't want to add any burden to her already difficult situation.

Qingfen had her home phone number transferred to the newly leased room just in case her daughter called home in the hope that she would not find she had moved out. She didn't want her daughter to get wind of the troubles she was suffering.

Qingfen wasn't able to sleep the first night after she moved in. The old couple both had asthma, getting up and walking around over and over again for a whole night. No wonder they were so willing to lease their home to Qingfen when they knew that she was a nurse. They had medical care for free.

# X

Sining had learned to smoke and she especially loved the long thin cigarettes given by Jianjian. With just a few puffs, she felt both excited and energetic.

After she entered the public university, Sining secretly swore to herself that she would work hard and finish her studies as soon as possible so that she could repay her mother for all the hardships she had suffered in bringing her up. College life could not be called tough, but most of the foreign students were weak in French. During classes, even with a lot of guessing, they could only understand about thirty percent of the courses. For the rest of the content, they had to rely on copying their French classmates' notes. Sining made a rule for herself that she had to study for three hours every night. When she got tired, she would have a smoke to pick herself up. When the cigarettes Jianjian had given her ran out, she went to school to inquire where she could purchase some of her own.

Lala told Sining in a mysterious way, "This kind of cigarettes is very expensive and you cannot get them in an ordinary store. But Jianjian knows a special supplier. They're fifty euros a pack."

"Fifty euros a pack? Do they put 'that kind of stuff' in them?" Sining cried in surprise.

"You are so clever, Miss Liu. What else can one sell at this price?" Lala said with indifference and a complete absence of concern. For her, even if it was 500 euros, it wouldn't matter at all.

For the whole day, Sining was in utter fright, because she was afraid that she might get addicted to this kind of cigarette and then fall into an unfathomable and unredeemable abyss. She tried all she could to keep her eyes away from Lala and Jianjian, but could not control a desire from the inside of her body. Near dusk, Sining was waiting at the red BMW, reluctantly producing 50 euros to get a pack of cigarettes from Jianjian. This money had been intended for food for the weekend and she had planned to go shopping in the supermarket after class. While she was waiting for the bus, Sining eagerly lit a cigarette and took a few puffs. She contentedly breathed out the smoke, forgetting that her refrigerator was completely empty.

Sining soon realized that besides herself, quite a few other Chinese students had also become victims of Jianjian's supply. Their parents would deposit money onto their bank cards, but how they spent the money was totally up to them. Initially, Sining felt ashamed and regretted her act, but when she found herself in a group, a sense of security emerged, because she knew she was not alone. Sining no longer forced herself to stay at home to study, but rather hung along with Lala and Jianjian. She would follow them wherever they went and of course, the vacant seat in the BMW was always there for her.

The night before Easter Sunday, Sining went with Lala and Jianjian to an open-air bar. Some other Chinese students also came. While they drank and talked, a tall young man asked Jianjian for one of his cigarettes, but Jianjian refused and said, "You must first pay for the two packs you had the last time." Insulted and angry, the guy picked up the wine glass and threw it in Jianjian's face.

Lala was with Sining and another few girls at a round table, but seeing her boyfriend bullied by another guy, she picked up her glass and hurled it back in the other guy's face. He, in turn came staggeringly at Lala, seized her by the shoulder and violently pushed her to the ground. The back of Lala's head hit the curb of the road with a dull noise and Lala gave out a bitter scream and rolled onto the road.

The bartender called the police immediately and both a police car and an ambulance soon arrived. The last scene Sining saw was Lala being carried away with her arms loosely hanging down.

Sining dashed like mad for the ambulance and cried with all her strength, "Lala, are you all right?"

A policeman grabbed Sining by the arm, "Miss, please come with us." Sining and all the students were brought to the police station tossed some light on what had happened.

Lala stopped breathing on the way to the hospital—two weeks shy of her 19th birthday.

Sining didn't know how long she had stayed in the small room, only feeling that her mind was in a state of utter chaos. She had a strong wish to fumble for that pack of cigarettes, but unfortunately her bag and other personal belongings had been taken away by the police. In a trance, Sining heard Madame Sophie's aged and hoarse voice, "Miss, come with me, I am now your guarantor."

Sining followed Madame Sophie into the police office and signed her name on a document and then went home in Madame's car. She cast a casual glance from the window of the car and happened to see Chen Lunian entering the police station. Sining patted at the window panes as if she found a savior, "Mr. Chen, go and save Jianjian immediately. They are all detained by the police."

Madame Sophie, who was driving, stopped Sining with a cold expression, "Miss, mind your own business. I'm having enough hassles having you as a tenant."

Normandy was normally a quiet area. But today the chaos hit all the papers. Headlines about loss of life due to fighting between overseas students aroused the attention of the whole country. The local media were wild with joy, and took turns to interview Miss Liu Sining the principal witness. Madame Sophie had to tie her two huge dogs at the door to avoid harassments from reporters.

A few days later, another piece of eye-catching news appeared on the front pages of the French mainstream media: The Normandy Business School was suspected of fraud in its admission process. The main protagonist in the story was Chen Lunian, who, in collusion with the French vice-president in charge of registry, had admitted foreign students who did not qualify for entry to the college and asked for bribes of various amounts from students. The French media even called Chen

Lunian and the vice-president "overseas student extortionists" and deplored the theft from both French tax payers and parents of the students.

The French court soon registered the case for investigation and both Sining and Jianjian were summoned by the prosecutors more than once. The Normandy Business School soon decided to expel Sining and other students who had not sat for the public matriculation test or were not qualified for a public university, and also had them registered with the immigration bureau.

## XI

A bad incident of food poisoning occurred in the primary school near the community hospital and all afternoon Qingfen had been so busy taking care of more than ten very sick children, she hadn't even had a chance to have a drink of water. Near night, after the condition had been stabilized, Qingfen went back to the nurse's station. Her knees became weak and limp and she sank into a chair. She had been working continuously for more than ten hours.

Her cell phone in the pocket of her nurse uniform vibrated. Even though it was on silent, it gave Qingfen a fright. Who would call her at midnight? As she looked down at her phone, she found it was her daughter calling. But after several hellos from her, no more responses came from the other end. An unexpected ominous portent suddenly engulfed her. Qingfen seemed to hear her daughter's low sobs.

"Sining, are you all right? My good daughter, baby, don't worry. Mom is here. Tell me what has happened right now." Qingfen anxiously shouted into the cell phone.

"Mom, I want to come home, home, home …" After a series of painful and heartbroken screams, she burst out crying loudly. She then switched off her cell phone, cutting off her mother's anxious cries.

Qingfen guessed that something serious must have happened to her daughter, so she rushed out of the nurse's station onto the street in a trance and under the curtain of the night. A taxi slowly approached and the driver stuck out his head and asked, "Sister, want a taxi?" Qingfen unconsciously opened the door and got in, not knowing where to go. The driver couldn't make head or tail of what had happened and inquired, "Sister, are you in trouble and looking for a friend for help? Where does your friend live? Let me drive you there."

The first person she thought of turning to was Lianyin. But she soon dismissed this ridiculous idea. Lianyin had brought his wife and child to Shanghai and had settled down in her old apartment, what possible reason did she have to disturb the peace and quiet of a family which was totally unrelated to her? Fortunately, she still had Miss Ye's cell phone number in her phone. After a short moment of hesitation, she finally punched in that number.

Miss Ye woke up with a start. After Qingfen sobbed out her story on and off, Miss Ye consoled her, "Madam Yang, take it easy. Go and wait at our agency, and I'll drive there right away."

The taxi driver dropped Qingfen off at the agency, and refused to take any money, saying that it was not a long distance. Before they parted, he left a comforting word, "Sister, Heaven will always leave a door open."

Miss Ye immediately started to contact the French side when she arrived at the office, but nobody was on Lunian's home phone and his cell phone was switched off. She turned on the computer, and there, waiting, was an email from Normandy.

After Qingfen heard Miss Ye's description of what was said in the email, she shouted, "Impossible! It is impossible! I sold our home and lost our family fortune to send her abroad for college. How could they expel her so rashly? What wrong did my daughter commit? The French people should be reasonable." After a few shouts, she suddenly became mute, and a stream of blood gushed out from her nostril. Miss Ye was greatly frightened and hurriedly put a towel toward Qingfen's face.

Qingfen had never tried gambling all her life. She did not even know how to play mahjong. But at this moment, she could completely and truly feel the horror of losing one's entire fortune in a night of gambling. She had lost her husband who shared everything with her, sold the home that provided her shelter and put all her hope on her daughter, but now she learned that her daughter had been expelled by the French university. Now nothing was left for Qingfen and she abruptly removed the towel from her face. She just wanted the blood to gush out wildly. When she ran out of blood, she would be able to have a good rest. She was too tired at heart and really wished to take a sleep and never wake up again.

At last, Miss Ye was able to find her friend in France. The friend promised to go to Normandy to see Sining the next day. Miss Ye wiped Qingfen's face clean and said, "Madam Yang, if you like, I'll help you apply for the visa right now. Bring your daughter back. As the saying goes, 'As long as the green mountains are there, one need not worry about firewood.' Your daughter is still young and there is still a long way to go for her. Many students who study abroad fail to obtain a college degree, but aren't they still successful?" Miss Yang felt deeply sorry for Qingfen and she was scolding herself at heart, wondering whether Qingfen and her daughter would make the same decision had she explained the risk plainly to them.

The Normandy Business School was ordered to

close indefinitely for "rectification." Chen Lunian and the French vice-president were under judicial investigation. Jianjian and other students who were expelled from the school successively came back to China. Only Sining remained in France at Madame Sophie's home. Since she had been expelled, she had been rooted in her room with bowed head all the time. When she saw others, all she could utter was invariably "I want to go home." These days, Madame Sophie stayed very close to Sining, rarely leaving her alone for a second. She had had no time to attend to her pets and her yard was an utter mess.

With the help of Miss Ye's friend, Qingfen made her way to Normandy to take her daughter home. Madame Sophie released a long sigh of relief, "Madame, now I give your daughter back whole. Please take her home, for there is nowhere better than home."

There was not a smile on her face, even when Sining saw her mother. She only repeated over and over, "I want to go home." Qingfen embraced her daughter tightly, "Sweetheart, Mom came just to bring you home. Let's go home."

There was a heavy downpour on the day Sining

and her mother left and after the rain, a colorful rainbow in the distant sky. Through the car window, Sining took a last glance at Normandy where she had lived for more than a year, but found the rainbow disappearing and huge dark clouds rolling and dashing in from the other side of the English Channel. Sining once again held her mother's arm in fright, whispering, "Mom, I want to go home."

A single teardrop dropped down Qingfen's icy-cold face.

## Stories by Contemporary Writers from Shanghai